Dear mouse friends,
Welcome to the world of

Geronimo Stilton

THE RODENT'S GAZETTE
EDITORIAL STAFF

...mme S.p.A., Via Galeotto del Carretto 10, ...Italia. International Rights @ Atlantyca ...n – Italy, foreignrights@atlantyca.it ...lantyca S.p.A.

...characters, and related indicia are copy- ...license of Atlantyca S.p.A. All rights ...author has been asserted.

...ogos are trademarks and/or registered

...English cheese. It is a registered trade- ...s' Association. For more information,

...d'America

...ncesco Castelli, and Christian Aliprandi ...ouse and Michela Battaglin

...ramontozzi

40

11 **12** 13 14/0

Geronimo Stilton
A learned and brainy
mouse; editor of
The Rodent's Gazette

Thea Stilton
Geronimo's sister and
special correspondent at
The Rodent's Gazette

Trap Stilton
An awful joker;
Geronimo's cousin and
owner of the store
Cheap Junk for Less

Benjamin Stilton
A sweet and loving
nine-year-old mouse;
Geronimo's favorite
nephew

ISBN-13: 978-0-545-02137-1
ISBN-10: 0-545-02137-5

Copyright © 2006 by Edizioni Pie
15033 Casale Monferrato (AL),
S.p.A. Via Telesio 22, 20145 Mil

English translation © 2009 by A

www.atlantyca.com

Text by Geronimo Stilton
Original title *La Corsa Più Pazza*
Cover by Giuseppe Ferrario
Illustrations by Danilo Barozzi, Fr
Graphics by Merenguita Gingerm

Special thanks to Beth Dunfey
Special thanks to Lidia Morson T
Interior design by Kay Petronio

12   11

Printed in the U.S.A.
First printing, April 2009

Geronimo Stilton
A learned and brainy
mouse; editor of
The Rodent's Gazette

Thea Stilton
Geronimo's sister and
special correspondent at
The Rodent's Gazette

Trap Stilton
An awful joker;
Geronimo's cousin and
owner of the store
Cheap Junk for Less

Benjamin Stilton
A sweet and loving
nine-year-old mouse;
Geronimo's favorite
nephew

Geronimo Stilton

THE RACE ACROSS AMERICA

Scholastic Inc.

New York   Toronto   London   Auckland   Sydney
Mexico City   New Delhi   Hong Kong   Buenos Aires

ISBN-13: 978-0-545-02137-1
ISBN-10: 0-545-02137-5

Copyright © 2006 by Edizioni Piemme S.p.A., Via Galeotto del Carretto 10, 15033 Casale Monferrato (AL), Italia. International Rights @ Atlantyca S.p.A. Via Telesio 22, 20145 Milan – Italy, foreignrights@atlantyca.it

English translation © 2009 by Atlantyca S.p.A.

www.atlantyca.com

GERONIMO STILTON names, characters, and related indicia are copyright, trademark, and exclusive license of Atlantyca S.p.A. All rights reserved. The moral right of the author has been asserted.

Published by Scholastic Inc.
SCHOLASTIC and associated logos are trademarks and/or registered trademarks of Scholastic Inc.

Stilton is the name of a famous English cheese. It is a registered trademark of the Stilton Cheese Makers' Association. For more information, go to www.stiltoncheese.com.

Text by Geronimo Stilton
Original title *La Corsa Più Pazza d'America*
Cover by Giuseppe Ferrario
Illustrations by Danilo Barozzi, Francesco Castelli, and Christian Aliprandi
Graphics by Merenguita Gingermouse and Michela Battaglin

Special thanks to Beth Dunfey
Special thanks to Lidia Morson Tramontozzi
Interior design by Kay Petronio

12 11   40   11 12 13 14/0

Printed in the U.S.A.
First printing, April 2009

TO: GERONIMO STILTON

It had been a **stressful** day at the office. By six o'clock, I was exhausted!

As I scampered home, I thought about taking a nice, relaxing bath in a tub of **cheese-scented** bubbles. Ahhh . . .

Oops, I almost forgot to introduce myself! My name is Stilton, *Geronimo Stilton*. I am the publisher of the most famouse newspaper on Mouse Island, *The Rodent's Gazette*. I also love to read and write books.

When I arrived in front of my mouse hole at 8 Mouseford Lane, I noticed something unusual on the front stoop. Curious, I bent down to check it out. It was a package.

Could it be for me? I hoped so! I **love** getting packages in the mail.

I picked it up and read the tag. It *was* for me!

"Hmmm. Who could've left this here?" I wondered aloud.

I picked up the B O X and went inside.

To: Geronimo Stilton
8 Mouseford Lane
New Mouse City
Mouse Island 13131

Then I ripped off the brown **wrapping** paper.

Once I got the box open, I was dumbfounded and a little disappointed. Bicycle **HanDLeBaRs**?!

WHO HAD SENT THEM TO ME?

MORE IMPORTANT, WHAT WAS I GOING TO DO WITH BICYCLE HANDLEBARS?

You see, I'm hardly what you'd call a sportsmouse. My favorite hobby is *curling* up with a good book. So why would someone send me bicycle handlebars?

It was a **MYstERy**.

TWO PEDALS?!

The next day, I woke up bright and early. I went into the bathroom and took a warm shower, just like always. Then I headed into the kitchen and got myself an apple and a nice cup of **HOT** cheddar, just like always. I left my house whistling, just like always, and headed to my office at *The Rodent's Gazette*.

On my way out, I **TRIPPED** over something on the front stoop. Before I could stop myself, I **fell** flat on my face! Ouch!

I got up slowly, rubbing my tender snout.

That's when I realized I had tripped over another package.

I read the tag:

To: Geronimo Stilton
8 Mouseford Lane
New Mouse City
Mouse Island 13131
P.S. What are you waiting for? Open it now!

I decided to do as the tag said. I went back into my mouse hole and tore open the package. Inside were two bicycle pedals!

TWO PEDALS?!

WHO HAD LEFT THEM FOR ME?

MORE IMPORTANT, WHAT WAS I GOING TO DO WITH TWO BICYCLE PEDALS?

It was a conundrum.

A Bicycle Helmet?

I was still thinking about the two anonymouse packages as I headed toward my OFFICE. But as soon as I walked through the door to *The Rodent's Gazette*, my staff swarmed around me. There was no time to ponder the mystery. In fact, by the end of the day I had completely forgotten about the **WEIRD** gifts I had received.

Late that afternoon, I CHECKED the last page of *The Rodent's Gazette*, *signed* several important documents, and wrote a few chapters of my new book.

When I arrived at my mouse hole, I found yet **ANOTHER** package with the same tag!

I scurried inside and ripped open the package as fast as I could. By now, I was determined to get to the bottom of all this.

To: Geronimo Stilton
8 Mouseford Lane
New Mouse City
Mouse Island 13131
P.S. Open this package immediately, you cheesehead!

It was a bicycle **HELMET**.

WHO HAD LEFT IT FOR ME?

MORE IMPORTANT, WHAT WAS I GOING TO DO WITH A BICYCLE HELMET?

It was a puzzle.

As I mulled it over, the 🄳🄾🄾🅁🄱🄴🄻🄻 rang. I went to the door. "Who is it?" I called.

No one answered. But then the door *BURST* open!

7

I HOPE YOU LIKE RIDING BICYCLES!

"Howdy, Geronimo! Happy to see me?" The mouse on the other side of the door gave me a hearty slap on the back. **Ouch!**

It was my friend **Bruce Hyena**. Bruce is the sportiest mouse I know.

"I've got a proposition for you, Geronimo," Bruce said. "It's something that needs **LOTS** and **LOTS** and **LOTS** of enthusiasm. You like riding bikes, right? If you do, slap me five!"

Timidly, I slapped him five. **YOW!** He slapped me so hard, my whole paw ached!

"I do like to ride bikes." I said. "I've got a really *nice* bicycle that has a wicker basket in the front. It's perfect for carrying a picnic and a book —"

"WICKER BASKET?!" Bruce said incredulously. "I meant a **RACING BIKE**, you **cheesehead**! You know, a serious bicycle — a bike for **real mice**! Not a bike for a spin in the park!"

I smiled. "Bruce, you know what a bookmouse I am. I like a quiet life."

"Quiet life? You'll have to squeak good-bye to that for a while! You see, I've already signed you up for the **RACE ACROSS AMERICA!**"

"The Race Across America?" I said blankly. "But that sounds like —"

"That's right! You bet!" Bruce interrupted.

"We'll be riding our bikes across the **WHOLE** country! No sweat, right?"

"But . . . but . . ." I sputtered. My head began to spin. "Rat-munching rattlesnakes! Do you know how big America is?"

"Of course I do!" cried Bruce, giving me another hearty slap on the back. "A trip like that should be a breeze for a couple of buff sportsmice like us, right, Champ?"

I opened my mouth to protest, but no sound came out. I think I was in shock.

Ha! Ha! Haaa!!!

My head began to spin, spin, spin, spin, spin . . . spin, spin, spin, spin

THE HISTORY OF THE BICYCLE

The first bicycle was invented in 1861 by the French mechanic Ernest Michaux. It was called the **velocipede**. The velocipede had pedals mounted on a large front wheel. This helped riders travel very fast with very little effort.

The **modern bicycle** was born in 1880 with the invention of the *chain*, which transfers power from the bicycle's pedals to its wheels. A few years later, **rubber tires** were added. Tires made riding a bike a lot more comfortable. Before they were invented, cyclists rode on wheels made of wood or iron.

Today **racing bicycles** have narrow tires, curved handlebars, and most important, a **gear** mechanism that makes it easier to pedal up even the steepest hills. These bikes are made from ultralight materials, like carbon fiber or titanium. Every piece of the bicycle is designed to be as light as possible to help improve the rider's speed.

What is the...
RACE ACROSS AMERICA?

The Race Across America is the longest and most strenuous bicycle race in the world. It's an ultra-marathon race that's more than 3,000 miles long. Cyclists pedal for nine to twelve consecutive days, some resting only one to three hours every day. The race starts on the West Coast, near San Diego, California, and ends on the East Coast. The exact finish line changes from year to year, but was most recently in Annapolis, Maryland.

The race requires an incredible amount of physical energy, but mental concentration is also absolutely essential. In fact, some people believe that mental concentration is the most important factor in the race.

Cyclists climb more than 100,000 feet along the racecourse. Participants must pedal across the California and Arizona deserts, enduring brutal temperatures that can reach as high as 105 degrees Fahrenheit. Then racers must face the Rocky Mountains, the plains of Kansas, and the Appalachian Mountains on their way to the East Coast. It's easy to see why the Race Across America is considered one of the most difficult racing challenges in the world.

THE MOST CHALLENGING RACES IN THE WORLD

1. **The Race Across America** is a 3,000-mile bicycle race across the United States.

2. **The Vendée Globe** began in 1989. In this famous race, sailboats sail around the world without stopping. The race begins and ends in France.

3. **The Iditarod Trail Sled Dog Race** is an annual sled dog race in which mushers with teams of ten to sixteen dogs cross Alaska from east to west, covering 1,161 miles in eight to fifteen days.

4. **The Ironman World Championship** is the world's oldest, longest, and most prestigious triathlon. The first Ironman competition was held in Waikiki, Hawaii, on February 18, 1978. Competitors must swim 2.4 miles, bike 112 miles, and run 26.2 miles.

RECORDS FOR THE RACE ACROSS AMERICA

Riders can participate in the Race Across America as individuals or as part of a group. An individual cyclist can travel about 430 miles a day in approximately 22 hours. In the race's 26-year history, fewer than 200 solo cyclists have finished the race.

- In 1986, Pete Penseyres set a world record for biking 3,107 miles in 8 days, 9 hours, and 47 minutes.
- A cyclist burns an average of 300 calories an hour (a total of 7,000 calories a day) during the race!

UNCLE GERONIMO, YOU'RE MY HERO!

I didn't remember saying yes to Bruce's plan. But I must have, because the next day, he pulled up in his car and whisked me off to begin my *TRAINING*.

"But, Bruce, I have to go to work today," I protested. "I'm needed at *The Rodent's Gazette*!"

"NONSENSE!" Bruce shouted. He dragged me into a bike store.

Before I knew it, he'd bought me an outfit made especially for *racers*: a cycling shirt, shorts, socks, and special bicycle shoes that latched onto my bike's pedals.

"Okay, let's get going," Bruce

said. "I want you to meet the **TEAM** that'll be by our side throughout the **RACE**. They're all great rodents. You'll see."

Bruce stopped in front of *The Rodent's Gazette*. The entire staff was waiting for me. They all seemed to know I was going to be riding in the **RACE ACROSS AMERICA**, and they'd come out to show their support.

My cousin Trap, my sister, Thea, and my little nephew, Benjamin, were at the front of the crowd. Benjamin ran to *hug me*.

"Uncle Geronimo, Bruce told us you're going to **AMERICA** to race! You're my hero! When I grow up, I want to be just like you."

I DiDn't KnoW WHat to say, so I just HUGGeD Him cLose. What could I do? I couldn't DISAPPOINT my favorite nephew.

It looked like I'd have to race whether I wanted to or not!

THE TEAM

Bruce took advantage of my moment of weakness to introduce me to the team.

"Hey there!" said a tall, thin mouse wearing a cowboy hat. "I'm **Tex**, the team's general manager. We've organized a system to monitor you at every step of the race. Put on these mini-microphones. They'll connect you to the camper that will follow you while you're racing."

Tex showed Bruce a tiny MICROPHONE that was attached to a long wire that extended from a small BATTERY.

"This way, if you need our help, we can get to you **FAST**," Tex explained.

Tex

TEAM N.M.C.

MOUSEY MACMOUSERSON
Known as the ranchero, Mousey is a cameraman planning to film the entire race for a documentary.

BUZZ
Buzz is Team N.M.C.'s mechanic. He's been crazy about bikes since he was nine years old. He runs a shop called The Bicyclist's Boutique.

SHORTY TAO
Bruce's cousin, a world karate champion. She works for *The Rodent's Gazette*.

TIGER
Our second van driver. A quiet, unassuming mouse like Geronimo.

NEW MOUSE CITY!

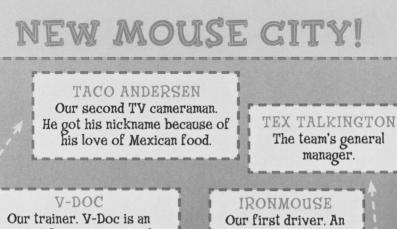

TACO ANDERSEN
Our second TV cameraman. He got his nickname because of his love of Mexican food.

TEX TALKINGTON
The team's general manager.

V-DOC
Our trainer. V-Doc is an expert at fixing sore muscles. All he has to do is take a quick look and he can tell exactly what the problem is.

IRONMOUSE
Our first driver. An athletic, well-rounded mouse who is also a triathlete.

MOUSITA MIDDLETON and BETTY SMARTMOUSE
Mousita and Betty work for *The Rodent's Gazette*. They organized the trip down to the teensiest, tiniest detail.

"Thanks, but I bet I won't need it," Bruce said. "I've been training for months."

Months? I gulped nervously.

Tex turned to me. "Sorry, Geronimo, but you'll have to carry an older version. We just gave out the last ultralight one."

"Oh, that's all right," I said. I wanted to show Bruce I could handle anything.

Then I saw the battery Tex wanted me to wear. IT WEIGHED AT LEAST SEVENTY-FIVE POUNDS!

Oh, what had I gotten myself into?!

"B . . . b . . . but how will I be able to carry this and pedal all those miles?" I stammered.

Bruce slapped my

"B . . . b . . . but how will I carry all this gear?"

shoulder. "**DON'T WORRY, CHAMP.** It's all part of training."

Training hadn't even begun, and I was already exhausted!

Tex smiled at me sympathetically. "You'll be just fine, Geronimo. Inside the camper we've got all kinds of things to help you rest and recover when you're not cycling. Plus our trainer, V-Doc, is the best!"

"Hmmm," V-Doc said thoughtfully. "Looks like I've got my work cut out for me! I can see you've got very small *MUSCLES*. Don't you worry, though. I'll fix you up in no time. Do you know what my motto is? *What doesn't bend gets broken!*"

I began to sweat.

Hmmm...

Before I could respond, Bruce had dragged me away to show me my bike. "Come on, Geronimo! Don't you want to meet your new best friend?" he said. "The two of you are going to be spending A LOT OF TIME together."

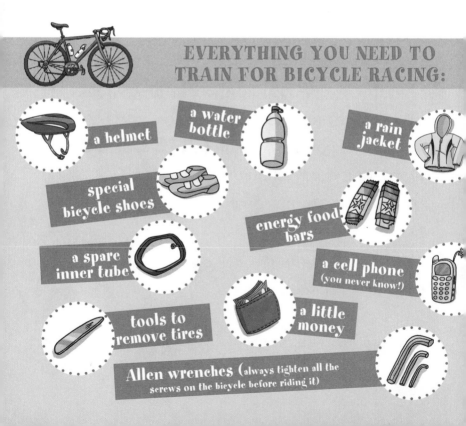

EVERYTHING YOU NEED TO TRAIN FOR BICYCLE RACING:

a helmet

a water bottle

a rain jacket

special bicycle shoes

energy food bars

a spare inner tube

a cell phone (you never know!)

tools to remove tires

a little money

Allen wrenches (always tighten all the screws on the bicycle before riding it)

GOOD FOR YOU, CHAMP!

Bruce showed me to my bike. It was a lot *fancier* than the one I used for picnicking in the park! It was sleek and silver.

"Come on, Champ! said Bruce. Let's take her for a spin to relax the paws."

That didn't sound so bad. I climbed on my new bike. Just sitting on it made me feel like a professional cyclist.

"Oh, I almost forgot to mention something," Bruce said. There are a few twenty-percent inclines on this course."

"Twenty percent? No sweat!" I replied enthusiastically. That sounded like nothing.

Bruce slapped my back so hard, he almost knocked me over. "Good for you, CHAMP!

We **PEDALED** for hours.

After 5 Miles, I was out of breath.

After 15 Miles, I had cramps in my paws.

After 25 Miles, my mouth was so dry, I had a hard time breathing.

After 50 Miles, my back was so sore, I wanted to scream.

After 75 Miles, I wanted to cry.

After 100 Miles, I fell off my bike!

Finally, we stopped for a break. "Bruce," I panted. "What does a twenty-percent incline mean?"

Bruce laughed. "Well, in bicycle racing, there are three types of inclines: the easy ones, the HARD ONES, and the **VERY HARD ONES**! A

After 5 miles

After 15 miles

After 25 miles

twenty-percent incline is **ONE OF THE HARDEST**. I thought you knew that, Geronimo!"

By the time we arrived HOME , I was totally exhausted. Holey cheese, I couldn't wait to get off my bike.

I hopped off, but the straps that held my paws onto the pedals didn't release. **I TOPPLED OVER** and landed right on my poor tail!

Bruce looked down at me. "You know what, Champ?" he said confidently. "Maybe I'll go for another LITTLE RIDE. I can't sleep if I don't ride at least a hundred and fifty miles."

He waved cheerfully and pedaled off.

Bruce Hyena is a good friend, but I'd never been so glad to see him go.

After 50 miles   After 75 miles   After 100 miles

WHAT IF WE MOVE MR. X . . .

The two weeks of training were more **PAINFUL** than anything I could have imagined. But whenever I thought of giving up, I just remembered the look in Benjamin's eyes when he'd called me his hero and I kept at it.

Finally, the big day came. The entire N.M.C. **TEAM** was ready!

We met at New Mouse City's airport with our enormouse **SUITCASES**. We had to take apart our bikes and put them in special cases so they could fit on the plane.

We boarded the plane to find every seat was taken. The team was spread **ALL OvER thE PLACE**. That didn't

make Bruce happy at all. He was determined to sit **NEXT TO ME** so we could talk strategy!

"I'll ask somebody to switch seats with me," he offered.

"Oh, it's okay, Bruce," I said. I thought about the book I'd packed in my carry-on bag. I'd been so **BUSY** cycling, it felt like ages since I'd curled up with a good story.

"Listen, Champ, this may be our last chance to B R A I N S T O R M before the race," Bruce said. "We've got sixteen hours, and we're going to need every minute!"

Bruce asked the mice on either side of both our seats to **switch** with one of us. But no one would do it. So Bruce pulled out a scrap of paper and started to figure out **ALL KINDS OF WAYS**

to move **RODENTS** around so we could sit together.

"Look, Geronimo! If we move Mr. X here, then we can switch Mrs. Y here and seat 21 will be EMPTY. Then we can ask Mr. Z to change with Mrs. H. Then there's Mr. Q, who will only sit in a window seat. Can you believe the nerve of that rodent?!"

Pretty soon, everyone on board was complaining about Bruce. The flight attendant had to tell him to take his seat and quiet down.

I breathed a sigh of relief and I pulled out the final *Ratty Potter* book. At last, some peace and quiet!

But not for long. After a few hours, Bruce appeared at my side. "Psst! Cheesehead!" he hissed. "Don't forget to keep your paws loose! Try these exercises."

EXERCISES TO STRETCH YOUR LIMBS WHILE FLYING

HEAD: Massage your temples.

EYES: Place your fingers on your eyelids and press gently.

NECK: Turn your head from right to left, then from left to right.

SHOULDERS: Raise your shoulders all the way up to your ears.

BACK: Bend your torso all the way to your knees.

ARMS: Bend one arm behind your head and push it down with the other.

FEET: First raise your toes, then your heels.

LEGS: Pull each knee toward you.

WAIST: Twist to the right, then to the left.

HOPE HOSPITAL

A few hours later I was starting to feel a little lonely. I peered around to look for my teammates. Bruce caught my eye and came over to talk to me.

"Geronimo, I've got something to tell you," he began. I'd never seen my cheerful friend look so SERIOUS!

"What is it, Bruce?" I asked. "You know you can tell me anything."

"Well, I've been volunteering for a while at Hope Hospital," he said. I was surprised. I had no idea he'd been volunteering. But it made sense. Bruce Hyena likes to talk big, and he has a big heart to match.

"I work in the wing where children with leukemia are hospitalized," Bruce went on.

"Leukemia is a disease that attacks blood cells and prevents them from fighting infections. So I was thinking — why don't we dedicate this race to the mouselets at **Hope Hospital**? I've lined up a few sponsors who will help us raise money. That way we can really help the **little heroes** who fight leukemia every day. We can do it, can't we, **Geronimo**?"

I was truly moved. I hugged my friend warmly. "Bruce, that's a great idea. We can definitely do it!"

I CAN'T SLEEP!

Another hour went by. The lights were dim.
I looked around me. Everybody was sleeping.
Even Bruce was snoring!

I knew I needed to rest a little
before we landed. After all, I had
quite an adventure in front of me.
So I closed my eyes and tried to
doze off. But NO LUCK!

I called the flight attendant
and asked for a cup of **hot cheddar**, thinking
that would help relax me. But NO LUCK!

At the end of the flight, I looked frazzled,
and Bruce looked like he'd just returned from
a trip to the *Restful Rodent* spa.

It wasn't fair.

I tried crossing my legs. NO LUCK!

I tried putting down my head on the tray in front of me. NO LUCK!

I tried hugging my knees and resting my head on them. NO LUCK!

I tried throwing my legs over the aisle armrest. NO LUCK!

I tried curling up into a fur ball. NO LUCK!

I tried pushing my knees on the seat in front of me. NO LUCK! NO LUCK! NO LUCK!

WELCOME TO SAN DIEGO!

We landed in San Diego, **CALIFORNIA**. I was totally zonked, and not just because I couldn't sleep.

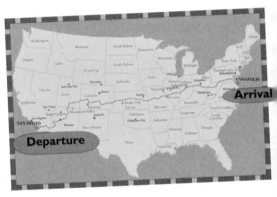

The **TIME DIFFERENCE** really made me feel terrible. You see, it was nine A.M. in San Diego, but back home in New Mouse City, it was **MIDNIGHT**!

As soon as we got to the hotel, **BUZZ**, the mechanic, immediately started putting our **bicycles** together.

While Buzz was **BUSY**, I figured

CALIFORNIA - SAN DIEGO

California is the third largest state in the United States, after Alaska and Texas. It is also the most populous. One of its largest cities is San Diego, which is located at the southern tip of the state on the Pacific coast.

The Spanish explorer Juan Rodríguez Cabrillo first sailed into San Diego Bay in 1542, hoping to find the wealthy cities known as Cibola. Today, if you walk along the waterfront, the Embarcadero, you will reach the Maritime Museum, which features one of the finest collections of historic ships in the world. One of the ships there, the *Star of India* (1863), is the world's oldest working ship.

In the heart of San Diego is Balboa Park. It is the largest urban cultural park in the United States. Founded in 1868, it is home to major museums, botanical gardens, performing arts centers, and the San Diego Zoo, which holds more than 4,000 animals.

I'd take a little ratnap in my room.

"GERONIMO! WHERE DO YOU THINK YOU'RE GOING!?" Bruce bellowed. He **BLOCKED** my path.

"Well, I had trouble sleeping on the plane, so I . . . I . . . thought . . ." I stammered.

"You thought you'd start the day with some solid training! Isn't that right? Good for you, Geronimo. I see the FIRE of enthusiasm in your EYES. I like it! Let's go for a nice jog."

Bruce is a mouse who knows what he wants and I could see that I wouldn't change his mind. So I dragged myself to my room to change into my tracksuit. Five minutes later, we were RUNNING along the waterfront.

Despite my exhaustion, being outdoors perked me up. AH, CALIFORNIA! The brilliant blue ocean seemed to stretch on forever. The seaside was gorgeous, with white sand that

sparkled in the warm sun. The beach was dotted with sunbathers and surfers.

It felt good to move my arms and legs again after being so cramped on that long flight. Bruce was right! Exercise was just what I needed. I **BOLTED** ahead, spurred on by the marvelous sights.

After a few minutes, I heard Bruce yelling, "... nimo ... Wa ... out for ... ole!"

I turned and shouted back, "What did you s — ?"

BANG!!! I ran smack into a pole!

Maybe jogging wasn't the best cure for jet lag, after all.

You Must Be the N.M.C. Crew!

Around **MIDMORNING**, the entire N.M.C. team gathered in our hotel lobby. We were on our way to the *CRUISE AMERICA CAMPING COMPANY* to pick up the camper the crew would use during the entire race.

Cruise America's owner, **MICKEY**, was waiting for us at the door. "You must be the N.M.C. CREW. I've got your camper right here. It's the last one left on the lot. You can sign the lease while I get the keys."

So Bruce *signed* the lease, and Mickey took us to our camper. It was enormouse, but it was dirty and dilapidated.

MICKEY

Bed

Table

Sofa Beds

Kitchen

Refrigerator

Bathroom

Shower

Night Table

Bed

Night Table

The rest of the team was as **gRoSSed** out as I was. But Shorty Tao just said, "Okay, gang! With a little elbow grease, we can make this dump spick-and-span! So roll up your sleeves and get your tails in gear!"

We all went to work. We washed the floor. We scrubbed the counters and the walls. We **shook**, **BEAT**, and *FLUFFED* the mattresses, pillows, and anything else we could shake, beat, and fluff.

After everything was spotless, we aired out the entire place. Finally, we went to pick up some cheese for the trip. I was starving!

By the end of the day, I was wiped out. But the camper was ready to tackle the RACE ACROSS AMERICA, and after a good night's sleep, I'd be ready, too!

ON YOUR MARK, GET SET, GO!

The big day had finally come! I woke up, nervous but excited.

At the starting line, the atmosphere was ELECTRIFYING. Everyone was bustling about, checking their bikes, fitting their helmets, and making sure their water bottles were filled. Some of the contestants were looking over the route on BIG MAPS.

Bruce, BUZZ, and I were busy tuning up our bikes so they'd be in tip-top condition.

AMERICA

We **inflated** the tires, **greased** the chains, **TIGHTENED** the screws on our handlebars, and **ADJUSTED** the seats so they were just right.

After the bikes were ready, V-Doc called us over. "Hey, Bruce! Geronimo! I'm going to give you guys a nice, **RELAXING** massage. Geronimo, you're first."

I scurried into the trailer. I love massages. But this turned out to be the least relaxing massage of my life! V-Doc *twisted* and **turned** me inside out, or at least that's what it felt like. By the time he was done, I could feel every muscle in my tail, and *not* in a good way.

Just as V-Doc started in on Bruce, we heard the loudsqueaker calling us to our places. No massage for Bruce, the lucky mouse! But I was too excited to care. It was time!

We put on our **helmets**. We'd decided I would **START** off the race. I was relieved because the first leg was the least difficult.

I joined the other cyclists at the starting line. Bruce slapped me on the back so

hard it was a miracle that I didn't fall over! "**READY, CHAMP?** Remember, pedal fast and smooth. Make sure you concentrate, and above all, keep a steady rhythm!"

I nodded. I couldn't believe the race was **FINALLY** beginning! I closed my eyes for a moment and thought about my dear nephew Benjamin, and how he'd said I was his **HERO**. I smiled and opened my eyes again. I was ready!

The voice on the loudsqueaker told us to mount our bikes.

"Ready? On your mark, get set,

GOOO!!!"

WELCOME TO
ARIZONA

I had just begun pedaling when the rest of the contestants passed me in a flash. Rodents from all over the world had come to compete in this race. It was truly an international **event**. As we passed one another, we smiled and wished each other good **luck**.

The open road stretched in front of me. The wind whistled through my fur. What an adventure! For the next several days, I'd be sharing the same *destiny* as rodents from countries all over the world. Our hearts would beat the same rhythm of **STRAIN AND PAIN**. We would all share in the same **excitement. It was thrilling!**

As we started out, I felt good. Whatever V-Doc had done to my **muscles** had really helped. Plus, I had spent the last few weeks training with Bruce and the rest of our team, and I was in better shape than I'd ever been. And last but not least, I had *eaten* a hearty breakfast of **oatmeal** right before the race began. (Before exercising, it's good to eat a meal rich in carbohydrates.)

The **landſcape** around me was breathtaking! I immediately settled into a steady pace. I smiled. I could hardly believe I was really here, competing in the RACE ACROSS AMERICA!

After a few hours, we turned onto *ROUTE 66*, the most famouse highway in the United States. I had already cycled almost 130 miles. In a little while, **Bruce** would switch with me.

As the sun started to sink, my paws began to ache. It was beginning to get **dark**. And I realized we'd entered the Arizona desert. There was a beautiful FULL MOON and nothing but sand for miles around!

ROUTE 66

Route 66 is the most famous highway in the United States. It was established in 1926 and is nicknamed the Mother Road. It begins in Chicago and ends in Los Angeles. Route 66 crosses eight states and runs for more than 2,000 miles. Jack Kerouac wrote about it in his famous book, *On the Road*. The highway was also immortalized in the song by Bobby Troupe, "(Get Your Kicks On) Route 66."

"What a beautiful night!"

CHEER UP, CHEESEHEAD!

I was getting HUNGRY, so I radioed **Tex** and **BUZZ**. They were following me in the team car. They pulled alongside me and handed me a cheddar sandwich.

Mmmm . . . cheese had never tasted so delicious! Biking hundreds of miles can really make a mouse hungry.

"Hey, Geronimo, is everything okay?" asked Tex. "You look tired."

"**Just a bit**," I replied. "I can ride a little farther."

"Do you need any more **waTeR**?" Tex asked.

A **STRONG**, **HOT** **WIND** was blowing.

It was 105 degrees and it was nighttime! It was hot, but I didn't feel thirsty.

"No, I'm okay," I told Tex.

But a few minutes later, I knew I was in trouble. I hadn't followed V-Doc's **INSTRUCTIONS**. He had told me to be sure to drink plenty of **FLUIDS**. Suddenly, I had a terrible hot flash! My lips were parched, I was completely dehydrated, and I had a **HiGH FeVeR**.

Cheese slices! I felt really sick! *I must not have had enough water to drink.*

The team car suddenly appeared alongside me. Tex and Buzz must have noticed that I had slowed down.

"Take heart, Geronimo," Buzz said. "Bruce will **RELIEVE** you."

That's when I realized the camper was on my other side.

Bruce scampered out. He looked all *fired up* and ready to go. "Cheer up, Cheesehead, it's my turn now." He reached out to give me a slap on the back. And then everything went black.

I HAD FAINTED!

When I came to, the first thing I saw was **V-Doc**. He was bending over me.

"Geronimo, did you drink enough water?" he asked. **"NO, DON'T TELL ME! I DON'T**

WANT TO KNOW! YOU DIDN'T, DID YOU?"

I was mortified. I really didn't know what to say. I felt like a mouselet who had been caught with his paw in the CHEESE JAR. And now I was being scolded. But I hadn't done it on purpose, I had just forgotten!

V-Doc looked at me sternly. "Geronimo, because of your mistake, Bruce has been PEDALING for the last EIGHT HOURS!"

I was shocked. "Jumping gerbil babies!

I've been out for eight hours?"

V-Doc nodded. "Bruce knew you weren't feeling well, so he asked not to be relieved. He told me not to wake you."

I felt TERRIBLE. I couldn't believe I'd let my FRIEND down like that!

I had to do something. **I needed to**

Bruce after **TWO HOURS**

Bruce after **FOUR HOURS**

Bruce after **EIGHT HOURS**

get well quickly so I could help Bruce!

"Please help me get better, V-Doc! I'll do whatever it takes."

V-Doc smiled. "**Good for you**, Geronimo. I knew you were tough! I'll give you a nice rubdown and you'll feel a lot better."

I had to do something.

MY TURN!

V-Doc was right! As soon as he finished my **MASSAGE**, I felt ready for anything. I strapped on my gear and dashed to the front of the camper.

Ironmouse was behind the wheel. "Signal the mice in the car to pull over. I need to **SWITCH** with my friend!" I told him.

"Done, Geronimo!" Ironmouse said with a *grin*.

I put on my bike helmet. Once the camper pulled over at the curb, I jumped out.

Bruce had stopped a few feet ahead of me. He was taking a deep drink from his water bottle. He turned and gave me a tired smile.

"HEY, CHAMP," he said slowly, "I'm glad you're feeling better!"

I hugged him. "Thank you for looking out for me, Bruce! You are a true friend. It's my turn now. So SLAP ME FIVE if you need to rest!"

Bruce grinned and slapped me five. I knew he must have been exhausted because it didn't hurt a bit.

I WINKED at him, then JUMPED on my bike and sped away.

THE GRAND CANYON!

I felt so much better. I pedaled mile after mile and I remembered to drink a lot of water. I was unstoppable!

Soon, **we arrived at the Grand Canyon.** Bruce was supposed to relieve me there, but I was determined to let him rest as long as possible. "I'll keep going," I told Tex. "Let Bruce rest a little longer!"

The road was filled with 20 percent inclines, but the view was **spectacular**. I should've been sweating my tail off, but the fantastic landscape made my aches disappear.

The walls of the canyons were very, very steep. Tex radioed and told me that some of the canyons were as much as a mile deep! The ridges were carved by thousands of years of ice, rain, and **WIND**.

I couldn't believe how lucky I was to be seeing this incredible place with my own eyes. Of course, it was very hard work, but the breathtaking panorama made it all worthwhile.

I really *owed* it all to my best friend Bruce Hyena. If he hadn't trained me like a drill sergeant, I would have never had the strength to take on those steep hills!

The Grand Canyon is a World Heritage Site in the state of Arizona. It is considered one of the wonders of the world. The canyon is a huge crack in a rock that averages 4,000 feet deep for its entire 277 miles. It is 6,000 feet deep at its deepest point and 15 miles wide at its widest point.

The canyon was formed by the path of the Colorado River over the past five or six million years. Over time, the canyon's walls grew wider and wider from summer thunderstorms and winter snowmelts.

The Colorado River cuts through the Grand Canyon. It begins in Rocky Mountain National Park, and flows approximately 1,450 miles to the Gulf of California in Mexico. Its waters change color from red to blue to green, depending on weather conditions and the different sediments in the riverbed.

Mousita

V-Doc

Buzz

Tex

Shorty Tao

Ironmouse

Tiger

Betty

As I zoomed along, I noticed a **CAMPER** by the side of the road. It was the **SWISS** crew.

My crew and I stopped to give them a paw. "What happened?" I asked.

The Swiss team manager looked anxious. "One of the camper's tires is **FLAT**," he replied. "If we don't change it fast, we'll have to pull out of the race!"

I turned toward Bruce and the rest of the crew. Everyone looked exhausted, but I could tell they knew what needed to be done.

Their **COURAGE**

and **determination** were inspiring.

"**All right, Rodents!** We've got the teamwork to make the dream work!" Bruce cried.

Faster than you can squeak "crumbling cheddar cheese crisps," we had that tire fixed, and the Swiss crew was ready to move! They thanked us ꝒꞄꝊ𝔽Ꞅ𝕊ꞓꝈꝏ, and sped off.

"Okay, Champ, it's time to switch. You can't keep this rodent out of the rat race any longer!" Bruce exclaimed. He gave me one of his famouse slaps on the back, and I almost fell over. **That's how I knew he was back to full strength.**

"Cheer up, Cheeseheads!" he told the rest of the team. "I feel stronger than ever. I'll fly over the next miles! Let's go!"

And with that, he was back on his bike and *RACING AWAY* as though all the cats on the Claw Islands were on his tail. He was more than a mile ahead of us before we caught up with him, and we were driving in the camper!

JUST LIKE THE OLD COWBOY MOVIES

I settled down in the camper's tiny kitchen for a nice snack. As I munched on a mozzarella ball, I looked out the window. We were in Monument Valley. The **red rocks** were bathed by the setting sun. What a beautiful sight! I felt like I was in an old **western**.

Buzz and I called Bruce on the radio.

"Howdy, partners!" Bruce shouted. I guess he shared my love of old cowboy movies. "It's very **WINDY** here. I can't go faster than fifteen miles an hour, even when I'm going downhill.

As we drove, Mousey and Taco, the two cameramen, had their cameras rolling, filming the spectacular scenery. And Bruce kept

ARIZONA
MONUMENT VALLEY

Monument Valley Navajo Tribal Park is 91,696 acres (143 square miles), and it's filled with many strange and unique sandstone

formations that have been shaped through time. They include buttes, mesas, canyons, and freestanding formations with enchanting names.

Ear of the Wind: If you listen carefully, you can hear the sound of the wind passing through the hole in this formation.

Eye of the Sun Arch: At a particular time of day, you can see the sun through the middle of the hole. It acts like a natural clock.

The most famous formations are the unmistakable Three Sisters, which appear in many Westerns.

SOME OF THE MOST FAMOUS WESTERNS OF ALL TIME WERE SHOT RIGHT IN MONUMENT VALLEY:

Stagecoach (1939)

My Darling Clementine (1946)

Fort Apache (1948)

She Wore a Yellow Ribbon (1949)

Rio Bravo (1950)

The Searchers (1956)

The Man Who Shot Liberty Valance (1962)

How the West Was Won (1982)

talking, even though he was still pedaling hard. He really is a mouse of steel. In fact, he started telling us j☺k☺s!

"Okay, listen to this one. There was a sportsmouse (just like me) who went to his friend, a bookmouse like Geronimo, and said, 'Want to do a marathon with me?' His friend asked, 'Hmm, how does it work?' So the sportsmouse explained, 'Well, we have to cover about twenty-six miles.' So the **bookmouse** squeaked, 'Fine, but you'll have to drive. I'm too tired!' Ha! Ha!"

I rolled my eyes. What can you do? That's Bruce for you!

FROM 120 DEGREES TO 40 DEGREES!

I lay down to sleep for a little while. It was important to rest while I could. I was so **exhausted**, I fell asleep as soon as my head hit the pillow! I woke a few hours later feeling rested and **refreshed**.

COLORADO

In the sixteenth century, Spanish explorers named the area Colorado because of its red-colored earth. Colorado means "red" in Spanish. Colorado has fifty-four mountain peaks that are more than 14,000 feet high.

Colorado National Monument preserves 32 square miles of canyons and mesas sculpted from years of erosion. A few miles west is Miracle Rock, a huge

sandstone outcropping perched on a narrow cliff. It may be the biggest wobbly rock in the world.

120 DEGREES

It was time for me to get back on my bike. Just my luck — we were right at the beginning of a huge mountain range. We had crossed the COLORADO border!

I'd gotten used to the heat in the desert, where it was *120 DEGREES* Fahrenheit. But here in the mountains, the temperature dropped down to **40 DEGREES**. Rat-munching rattlesnakes! It made the work of pedaling the bike twice as hard.

I panted and panted as I pushed one paw in front

40 DEGREES

of the other. Holey cheese, how I wished it was still Bruce's turn! The *steep* road up the Colorado mountains was more than **THIRTY-FIVE MILES** long! I thought it would never end.

As I huffed and puffed along, the weather suddenly turned from **SUNNY** to cloudy. *Brrrr!* Now it was even colder!

Just then . . . **PSSST!!!!**

I got a **flat tire**!

"Go, Geronimo!" Before I even had a chance to radio the crew, **BUZZ** hopped out of the car and scampered over to me. Before you could squeak "chewy cheddar cheese chunks," he'd **FIXED** my tire!

HOW TO CHANGE A FLAT TIRE ON A BICYCLE

1. Remove the wheel from the bike.

2. Using an Allen wrench, carefully remove the outer tire. Then remove the inner tube and discard or patch it.

3. Take a new inner tube (or use your old, patched tube) and, after filling it with a little air from a bike pump, place it inside the rubber tire.

4. Insert the rim of the rubber tire back into the wheel.

5. Use your bike pump to fill the tire with air. Then place the wheel back onto the frame of the bike.

LAUGHTER IS THE BEST MEDICINE

After a while, we arrived in **DURANGO**, a beautiful town in the mountains. The landscape was dotted with pine trees and junipers.

As I pedaled through the city, a real old-fashioned **steam engine train** puffed by, tooting its whistle.

I was starting to get tired, so Bruce and I switched again. Now we were heading on toward **KANSAS**. It was hard to believe, but we were almost halfway through the race! The farther we biked, the more excited Bruce and I became, even though we were both worn out.

The crew was weary, too, and they were feeling a bit **down**. So I decided to try to lift everyone's spirits the same way Bruce had, which was by telling jokes. I'd had plenty of time to think some up while I was racing along on my bike.

My grandfather, **William Shortpaws**, was a big believer in the power of laughter.

When my sister, **THEA**, and I were little, he always used to tell us, "Remember, mouselets, if you feel down, the best medicine is laughter!"

Soon we were all laughing our tails off.

Bruce heard the jokes through his headset, and he was laughing so hard, tears rolled down his snout. Even Tiger, who was driving the **CAMPER**, was doubled over with laughter.

All those chuckles and chortles made the next leg of the trip speed by. Soon we were in **DODGE CITY**, the heart of the Old West. Bruce had been riding his bike for several hours now, so it was **MY TURN AGAIN**.

DODGE CITY

DODGE CITY, KANSAS, WAS ONE OF THE MOST WELL-KNOWN CITIES IN THE OLD WEST. FOUNDED IN 1872, DODGE CITY WAS A MAJOR TRADING CENTER FOR TRAVELERS AND BUFFALO HUNTERS. TODAY, DODGE CITY HAS BEEN FAITHFULLY RECONSTRUCTED TO LOOK LIKE IT DID LONG AGO.

UPHILL STRUGGLES

Over the course of the race, I'd really started to enjoy riding at night. I spent the time plotting out my next few bestsellers. The gorgeous SCENERY really inspired a lot of great ideas! I was so busy BRAINSTORMING, I hardly noticed how hard I was working.

Sometimes I'd be so busy dreaming of books that I'd forget I wasn't really alone. Every once in a while, the mike connected to the camper would crackle.

"HEY, CHEESEHEAD, how's it going?" Bruce's

hearty voice boomed one evening.

Then Bruce grew serious. "Know what I was thinking, Geronimo? There have been so many enormouse hills in this race. That made me think of all the uphill struggles sick mouselets have to **Face** day after day. When you compare our struggles in this race to the ones the young mice at **Hope Hospital** are facing, it makes our hard work seem like nothing. If those mouselings can do it day after day, we can, too. Right, Champ?"

"Right, Bruce!" I responded. I smiled, even though he couldn't see me. That was why I liked Bruce Hyena so much—he was a great motivator!

PEDAL! PEDAL! PEDAL!

After a long night of pedaling, Bruce and I stood by the side of the road, getting ready to switch. Tex scampered up to us.

"Hey, you **road rats**. I was just on the radio with the organizers. There's only one TEAM ahead of us. And they're just sixty miles ahead! Do you know what that means?"

Bruce did. "**We can wiiiiinnn!**" he shouted. "Geronimo! We can do it! We've got to do it for all those mouselings at the hospital."

THERE WAS NO TIME TO LOSE! Bruce leaped on his bike and raced away.

Bruce and I became two lean, mean biking machines, switching every two hours.

ST. LOUIS

The last few states flew by. When we reached St. Louis, Missouri, we saw an authentic riverboat docked on the Mississippi, right in front of the famouse high steel arch. Then we arrived in *Indianapolis*, where the Indy 500 takes place.

MISSISSIPPI RIVER

INDIANAPOLIS

Next we pedaled hard toward **OHIO**, concentrating on the rhythm we needed to overtake the racers ahead of us.

PEDAL! PEDAL! PEDAL!

OHIO

The distance separating us from the first-place team was getting shorter and shorter. Soon we were only a few miles from ANNAPOLIS, MARYLAND, where the finish line was waiting.

But just when I saw a sign that said ANNAPOLIS 20 MILES, something bad happened. Crusty kitty litter, it was BAD.

No, wait a minute. The word *bad* doesn't do justice to how TERRIBLE it was. It was awful. Ghastly, horrific, and dreadful. One might even say it was DISASTROUS!

It happened like this. I was pedaling along with Tex and Buzz behind me in the team car. At this point, we'd been pushing ourselves nonstop for more than twenty-four hours. And that's how Tex and Buzz turned onto the WRONG road without me noticing it.

No big deal, right? Well, the race's rules

say each team's car has to escort its cyclists to the finish line in **Annapolis**. Otherwise, that team is disqualified!

Geronimo··

A BREATHLESS FINISH!

When I realized the car wasn't behind me anymore, I almost fainted. It's a good thing my shoe clips held me on the bike.

RANCID RAT HAIRS, WHAT COULD I DO? WHAT? WHAT

I turned the bicycle around as quickly as I could, Then I began *pedaling harder* than I ever had before. I didn't use the brakes once. I was like the wind!

I passed my crew in the camper. I'd radioed them to tell them what had happened, and they'd stopped to cheer me on.

Bruce was standing outside the camper. He was cheering, "GO, GERONIMO! YOU CAN DO IT!!!"

Finally, I saw a dot faraway on the horizon. It was coming toward me. It was our team car.

"Go, Geronimo, go!" Tex shouted.

Faster than you can squeak "flying cheese sticks dipped in fondue," I'd turned around and started sprinting in the OPPOSITE DIRECTION. We were back on track and heading toward the FINISH line!

I'd never pedaled faster in my life.

My mouth was **dry**, my paws were **ACHING**, and sweat was dripping down my fur right into my eyes.

But there it was! The FINISH line! And there, just a few yards away from it, was the cyclist from the team ahead of us!

I was so close, I knew I could catch up with him. This was the FINAL STRETCH! There were all the fans! There was my crew about to cross the FINISH line!

At that moment, I tried to accelerate, but my front tire hit a rock and . . .

Suddenly, I was **FlYiNGGGGGGG!!!!!!!!!**

FRIENDS TOGETHER! MICE FOREVER!

Here's what happened next.

Because of that rock, I **FLIPPED** through the air and landed right on top of my opponent's head. Then I **tumbled** onto the FINISH line! That flying leap onto the FINISH line helped me finish first!

WE HAD WOOOOOOOOOOOOOOON!!!!

Bruce and the entire team ran to hug me. They were so thrilled it ended up being more of a tackle than a hug. Soon the whole team was piled on top of me. But I didn't care.

"Yeaaaah!" shrieked Tex. "We did it!"

Bruce was hugging me so hard, I thought he was going to crush my ribs. "Cheesehead, when I told you the trick to winning was to arrive a second before the rodent in first place, I never thought you'd take me literally!" He gave me another tail-crunching embrace. "You really *are* a champ now!"

We hugged each other. Then I turned and embraced all the members of our crew one by one. This victory was for everybody, not just for Bruce and me. We never could have done it without our team.

At the AWARDS CEREMONY, we called the whole crew onto the stand with us to receive the trophy — Shorty Tao, Betty,

Mousita, Tex, V-Doc, Ironmouse, Tiger, Taco, Mousey, and Buzz!

Bruce winked at me. "You know, Geronimo, it took more than muscles to win this race. it took heart. And we've got lots of that on this team!"

I grinned at him. Then we joined hands with our teammates and shouted an old New Mouse City motto: *"Friends together! Mice forever!"*

HEY, CHEESEHEAD, ARE YOU SLEEPING?

That night, we had a **BIG** dinner to celebrate our victory. The next morning, we all boarded the plane for the flight back to New Mouse City. I couldn't wait to get home and tell Benjamin, Thea, and Trap all about our adventure.

"PSST! PSST! HEY, CHEESEHEAD!" Bruce whispered. "Slap me five if you're sleeping!"

I **rolled** my eyes. "Bruce, how I can slap you five if I'm really **sleeping**?"

"Good for you, Champ! I always knew you were a **BRAINY** mouse!"

Psst! Psst!

103

I smiled at him, then leaned my snout against my seat and tried to fall asleep.

I closed my eyes. In just a few hours, I'd be home in my nice, cozy mouse hole.

"PSST! PSST! HEY, CHEESEHEAD, ARE YOU SLEEPING?"

This time, I couldn't take it. "NO, I'M NOT SLEEPING! YOU WON'T LET ME!"

Uh-oh. I'd woken up the whole plane! And they were angrier than a mouse whose cheese has gone moldy.

"Shhhhh!"

"Who taught you your manners? A rabid tomcat?!"

"Be quiet!"

I was so EMBARRASSED, I wanted to crawl under my seat!

Bruce just ignored everyone and leaned

in closer. "Well, since you're not sleeping, I was thinking of something. What do you say about organizing another fun **ADVENTURE** with me?

I've got a bunch of great ideas. How about a **MOUNTAIN BIKE** trip through Patagonia? Or

a **trek** through the Valley of the Dinosaurs? Or we could do a nice **LITTLE RUN** up to the North Pole? Huh? What do you think?"

I had to **laugh**. "Just thinking about all those trips is making me tired, Bruce. Good night!"

THE REAL HEROES!

"Hey there, cousin!"

"Congratulations!"

"Uncle G!"

When our plane landed in New Mouse City, my entire **family** was waiting for me at the airport. In fact, half of New Mouse City had turned out to welcome us.

I WAS SO HAPPY TO BE HOME!

Benjamin jumped up to hug me. "Uncle G, I knew you could do it! **I LOVE YOU SO MUCH!**"

I kissed the tips of his whiskers, then gave him a tight squeeze.

My sister gave me a big hug. "I'm so proud

of you, Gerry Berry," she whispered.

Even my prankster cousin Trap looked happy to see me. I could tell he was busy trying to think up jokes to make — at my expense, of course. So before he could squeak, I gave him a Bruce-style slap on the back. That surprised him into silence!

I wanted to go straight home, but Bruce insisted we go to Hope Hospital first. And I was glad he did, because all the sick mouselings to whom we had dedicated our victory were waiting for us. They welcomed us like we were real heroes. But the fact was, *they* were the real heroes! That's why Bruce and I decided to give our little friends our trophy. Those mouselets were the ones who showed us real courage: the courage to face life!

Even though they were sick, these young mice found the strength to keep GOING.

They never let their suffering bring them down. For these young mice, every day was a new day, rich with **possibilities**.

Bruce presented the hospital administrator with a check for all the money we'd raised. I could see tears shining in her eyes. She looked so happy.

Looking at the *smiles* on those mouselets' snouts made me feel great. The RACE ACROSS AMERICA had been an enormouse challenge for me, but it was worth it. Bruce and I had an amazing adventure, and we were able to help some very special little mouselets. Given the chance, I knew I would do it again in a heartbeat!

Look for this fur-raising new adventure from my sister, Thea!

Geronimo Stilton

Thea Stilton
AND THE DRAGON'S CODE

SCHOLASTIC

THEA STILTON AND THE DRAGON'S CODE

I couldn't believe it when I, Thea Stilton, was invited to teach a journalism class at Mouse Island's most prestigious university! I had no idea that once I arrived, I would meet five amazing students. What's more, I didn't realize that another student would disappear—and the rest of us would have to help solve the mystery! Holey Swiss cheese, it was an incredible adventure!

And don't miss any of my other fabumouse adventures!

#1 LOST TREASURE OF THE EMERALD EYE

#2 THE CURSE OF THE CHEESE PYRAMID

#3 CAT AND MOUSE IN A HAUNTED HOUSE

#4 I'M TOO FOND OF MY FUR!

#5 FOUR MICE DEEP IN THE JUNGLE

#6 PAWS OFF, CHEDDARFACE!

#7 RED PIZZAS FOR A BLUE COUNT

#8 ATTACK OF THE BANDIT CATS

#9 A FABUMOUSE VACATION FOR GERONIMO

#10 ALL BECAUSE OF A CUP OF COFFEE

#11 IT'S HALLOWEEN, YOU 'FRAIDY MOUSE!

#12 MERRY CHRISTMAS, GERONIMO!

#13 THE PHANTOM OF THE SUBWAY

#14 THE TEMPLE OF THE RUBY OF FIRE

#15 THE MONA MOUSA CODE

#16 A CHEESE-COLORED CAMPER

#17 WATCH YOUR WHISKERS, STILTON!

#18 SHIPWRECK ON THE PIRATE ISLANDS

#19 MY NAME IS STILTON, GERONIMO STILTON

#20 SURF'S UP, GERONIMO!

#21 THE WILD, WILD WEST

#22 THE SECRET OF CACKLEFUR CASTLE

A CHRISTMAS TALE

#23 VALENTINE'S DAY DISASTER

#24 FIELD TRIP TO NIAGARA FALLS

#25 THE SEARCH FOR SUNKEN TREASURE

#26 THE MUMMY WITH NO NAME

#27 THE CHRISTMAS TOY FACTORY

#28 WEDDING CRASHER

#29 DOWN AND OUT DOWN UNDER

#30 THE MOUSE ISLAND MARATHON

#31 THE MYSTERIOUS CHEESE THIEF

CHRISTMAS CATASTROPHE

#32 VALLEY OF THE GIANT SKELETONS

#33 GERONIMO AND THE GOLD MEDAL MYSTERY

#34 GERONIMO STILTON, SECRET AGENT

#35 A VERY MERRY CHRISTMAS

#36 GERONIMO'S VALENTINE

And don't forget to look for

THEA STILTON AND THE DRAGON'S CODE

ABOUT THE AUTHOR

 Born in New Mouse City, Mouse Island, Geronimo Stilton is Rattus Emeritus of Mousomorphic Literature and of Neo-Ratonic Comparative Philosophy. For the past twenty years, he has been running *The Rodent's Gazette,* New Mouse City's most widely read daily newspaper.

Stilton was awarded the Ratitzer Prize for his scoops on *The Curse of the Cheese Pyramid* and *The Search for Sunken Treasure.* He has also received the Andersen 2000 Prize for Personality of the Year. One of his bestsellers won the 2002 eBook Award for world's best ratlings' electronic book. His works have been published all over the globe.

In his spare time, Mr. Stilton collects antique cheese rinds and plays golf. But what he most enjoys is telling stories to his nephew Benjamin.

THE RODENT'S GAZETTE

1. Main entrance
2. Printing presses (where the books and newspaper are printed)
3. Accounts department
4. Editorial room (where the editors, illustrators, and designers work)
5. Geronimo Stilton's office
6. Storage space for Geronimo's books

Map of New Mouse City

1. Industrial Zone
2. Cheese Factories
3. Angorat International Airport
4. WRAT Radio and Television Station
5. Cheese Market
6. Fish Market
7. Town Hall
8. Snotnose Castle
9. The Seven Hills of Mouse Island
10. Mouse Central Station
11. Trade Center
12. Movie Theater
13. Gym
14. Catnegie Hall
15. Singing Stone Plaza
16. The Gouda Theater
17. Grand Hotel
18. Mouse General Hospital
19. Botanical Gardens
20. Cheap Junk for Less (Trap's store)
21. Parking Lot
22. Mouseum of Modern Art
23. University and Library
24. *The Daily Rat*
25. *The Rodent's Gazette*
26. Trap's House
27. Fashion District
28. The Mouse House Restaurant
29. Environmental Protection Center
30. Harbor Office
31. Mousidon Square Garden
32. Golf Course
33. Swimming Pool
34. Blushing Meadow Tennis Courts
35. Curlyfur Island Amusement Park
36. Geronimo's House
37. New Mouse City Historic District
38. Public Library
39. Shipyard
40. Thea's House
41. New Mouse Harbor
42. Luna Lighthouse
43. The Statue of Liberty

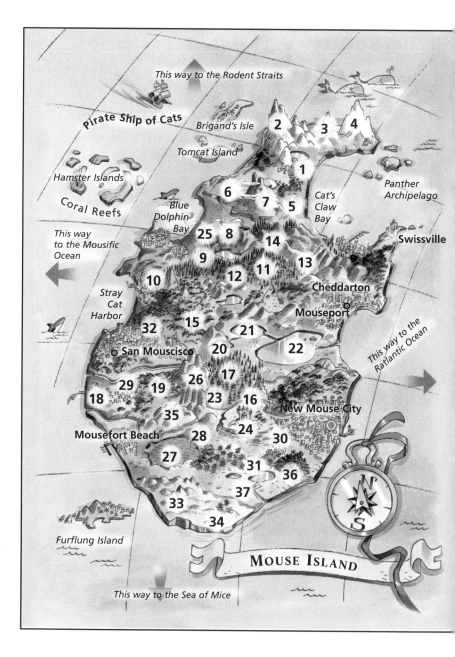

This way to the Rodent Straits

Pirate Ship of Cats

Brigand's Isle

Tomcat Island

2

3

4

1

Hamster Islands

Coral Reefs

Blue
Dolphin
Bay

6

7

5

Cat's
Claw
Bay

Panther
Archipelago

This way
to the Mousific
Ocean

25

8

14

Swissville

9

11

13

10

12

Cheddarton

Stray
Cat
Harbor

15

21

Mouseport

32

20

22

This way to the
Ratlantic Ocean

San Mouscisco

17

29

19

26

23

16

18

35

28

24

New Mouse City

30

Mousefort Beach

27

31

36

37

33

34

Furflung Island

N

W

E

S

MOUSE ISLAND

This way to the Sea of Mice

Map of Mouse Island

1. Big Ice Lake
2. Frozen Fur Peak
3. Slipperyslopes Glacier
4. Coldcreeps Peak
5. Ratzikistan
6. Transratania
7. Mount Vamp
8. Roastedrat Volcano
9. Brimstone Lake
10. Poopedcat Pass
11. Stinko Peak
12. Dark Forest
13. Vain Vampires Valley
14. Goose Bumps Gorge
15. The Shadow Line Pass
16. Penny Pincher Castle
17. Nature Reserve Park
18. Las Ratayas Marinas
19. Fossil Forest
20. Lake Lake
21. Lake Lakelake
22. Lake Lakelakelake
23. Cheddar Crag
24. Cannycat Castle
25. Valley of the Giant Sequoia
26. Cheddar Springs
27. Sulfurous Swamp
28. Old Reliable Geyser
29. Vole Vale
30. Ravingrat Ravine
31. Gnat Marshes
32. Munster Highlands
33. Mousehara Desert
34. Oasis of the Sweaty Camel
35. Cabbagehead Hill
36. Rattytrap Jungle
37. Rio Mosquito

Dear mouse friends,
Thanks for reading, and farewell
till the next book.
It'll be another whisker-licking-good
adventure, and that's a promise!

Geronimo Stilton

WORKS BY
NTOZAKE SHANGE

{PLAYS}

For Colored Girls Who Have Considered Suicide
When the Rainbow Is Enuf

Three Pieces

{NOVELS}

Sassafrass, Cypress & Indigo

Betsey Brown

Liliane: Resurrection of the Daughter

{POETRY}

The Love Space Demands: A Continuing Saga

Nappy Edges

A Daughter's Geography

Ridin' the Moon in Texas

{NONFICTION}

If I Can Cook / You Know God Can

{CHILDREN'S}

I Live in Music (poetry)

Whitewash (nonfiction)

12/

Gloria —
Happy Holidays!
Enjoy!

Ariel

IF I CAN (
YOU KNOW

If I Can Cook /
You Know God Can

NTOZAKE SHANGE

foreword by
VERTAMAE GROSVENOR

BEACON PRESS • BOSTON

BEACON PRESS
25 BEACON STREET
BOSTON, MASSACHUSETTS 02108–2892

BEACON PRESS BOOKS
ARE PUBLISHED UNDER THE AUSPICES OF
THE UNITARIAN UNIVERSALIST ASSOCIATION OF CONGREGATIONS.

03 02 01 00 99 98 8 7 6 5 4 3 2 1

TEXT DESIGN BY [sic]
COMPOSITION BY WILSTED & TAYLOR PUBLISHING SERVICES

LIBRARY OF CONGRESS CATALOGING-IN-PUBLICATION DATA

Shange, Ntozake.
If I can cook/you know God can / Ntozake Shange ;
foreword by Vertamae Grosvenor.
p. cm.
ISBN 0-8070-7240-0 (cloth)
1. Afro-American cookery. I. Title.
TX715.S526 1998
641.59'296073—dc21   97-35154

To Ellie, my mother, who could make a kitchen sing
and swing, make it a sacred or profane gathering,
a spooky, funny place, a refuge, a hallowed
midnight meeting with her daughter.

Contents

Contents

Recipes

Foreword

I FIRST MET ZAKI, as I shall call her from now on, in 1977 in Manhattan. It was a loft party and she was new in town. The room was filled with divas and "devos." And she still stood out with an energy that charged the room. Folks were asking, "Who is that?" Someone said, "She's that rainbow girl." Someone else said, "She's a gypsy." Others said, "She's a dancer, a poet." Uh uhhh, she is all that.

Many people were surprised that the "colored girl who was all that" was writing a cookbook. I wasn't. It was obvious from her earlier works, especially *Sassafras, Cypress & Indigo*, that a cookbook was simmering.

Zaki, in the tradition of Dumas, Colette, Amado, and other writers, understands the importance and connections of food and culture and how they are entwined in our everyday lives and manifest on our tables.

When I was growing up in Carolina low country, I didn't know the word *culture*. We just did the things we did the way we did them because that's the way they were done. We said what we said because we said it. I had no idea that many things we did in our everyday life reflected an African connection. When Gramama Sula said, "Yenna come nyam," we came to the table. I had no idea *nyam* was an African root word for "to eat" that can still be heard throughout the Americas. Besides, anything African was to be jettisoned into the Atlantic. Lots of people came to study the ways and customs of us low-country Geechee/Gullah folks, but no persons or books said, "It's a good thing. Honor the culture."

For my generation, it was a mark of shame to be like an African. But all praises to the food goddess. Now we have *If I Can Cook/You Know God Can*, a creative culinary celebration that compels us to hear the words, taste the spices, and feel the rhythms of Africa in the new world.

I don't know if she was born with it or if she developed it from a mighty culinary curiosity and/or life experiences, but for sure Zaki has a cosmopolitan palate. In this book she feasts on poetry and turtle eggs and spices in Nicaragua, and is apt at shopping the markets of Brixton in England or of Brooklyn, New York.

If I Can Cook/You Know God Can is testimony to the fact that although we may leave home, get rid of our accents, and change our names and diets, the aroma of certain foods will trigger warm memories and fill us with a longing and taste to return home. Once in Rome I passed someone's apartment and the smell of collard greens "gently stewing in the pot," as Langston Hughes wrote, made my eyes tear and knees buckle. I wanted to go home.

Zaki is a culinary traveler who knows when it's time to return to her roots. She can cook Brazilian rice and rice à la Carolina low country like her grandma Viola. This homegirl riffs on Barbadian flying fish, shark, and breadfruit and takes us back to the States to talk about harvesting sweet potatoes, fixing mustard greens, making chicken-fried steak, and growing watermelons. However, take note that she only be talking red watermelon, as in Oscar Brown Jr.'s vendor's cry, "Watermelon red to the rind!" Zaki makes it clear that she has no primal response to a "golden or blanched fleshed melon."

A personal culinary memoir, a travelogue with dashes of literature and pinches of music, this book is also a culinary history lesson, a history of what I call the Afro-Atlantic foodways. This heritage has been a confounding, embarrassing, and frightening inheritance for many. Zaki travels through it courageously.

She writes, "I remind myself that history, our history, mustn't scare me. Our history is the stuff rhumbas are made of, mambos, the jitterbug." *And* the mashed potato.

It's the history that until recently has been underappreciated and greatly distorted. Like urban legends the myths become ludicrous narratives. There are two myths that make me madder than a wet hen, and I want to beat them with a mallet:

1. "Slaves brought foods with them during the Middle Passage."

This culinary falsehood is so widely believed that some food historians have written that the Africans carried luck, bringing sesame seeds in their ears to the new world. Yes, certain foods did travel the Middle Passage to the Americas but they were not carried in the ears or baggage of kidnapped Africans.

2. " 'Soul food'—collard greens, okra, cornbread, pig's feet, etc.—grew out of 'massa's' leftovers and is a unique non-cuisine, eaten only by blacks in the southern United States."

So what are those delicately flavored, thin shiny green ribbons served in Rio every Saturday along with the feijoada?

Oh, you say couve, we say kale, or collards . . . and in Bahian is that okra I spy in your shrimp carúrú?

You say those fritters frying are made out of black-eyed peas and you call them acaraje?

Uhmm Ola told me they call them akara in Lagos.

And we make something like that out of cornmeal and call them hush puppies.

You say you been making bread out of corn for centuries in Vera Cruz?

And those fried, stuffed pig's feet I had at that little Left-Bank bistro were from what region of France?

In *If I Can Cook/You Know God Can* Zaki reminds us of those culinary connections and expands our culinary horizons. She will tempt you to eat a big slice of avocado and down it with beer. And then she'll suggest you serve wheatmeat with organic brown rice when company is coming. And she is bold! In the nineties, the decade of lattes and rice cakes, where the f-word (*fried*) is unspeakable, she gives a recipe for french-fried chitlins. She doesn't insist that you eat what she eats or fix it her way, though. She understands it's your kitchen. But no matter, she's so engaging, she'll make you pause and consider what you put in your mouth.

Zaki has taken the lid off the cultural melting pot—and what a splendid aroma! *If I Can Cook/You Know God Can* is a mouthwatering, smoking-hot, nourishing stew. It's being served on a table handcrafted and carved in Haiti. There are daylilies from Savannah, coxcombs and marigolds from Oaxaca, and wildflowers from across the Americas. The centerpiece is a cornucopia of coconuts, cassava, plantain, mangoes, papaya, bananas, eggplants, breadfruit, true yam, sweet potatoes, sugarcane, starfruit, persimmons, and other delectables. It's dished up in earthenware bowls and eaten with silver-handled wooden spoons. There's crusty golden pain de la maïs in Gullah sweetgrass baskets kept warm with heavy linens trimmed with delicate lace from Guadeloupe, and crystal glasses of sweetened iced tea.

So yenna come nyam! Enjoy! I did and you know God can!

VERTAMAE GROSVENOR

Learning to Be Hungry /
Holdin' On Together

I N THE SUMMER OF 1987, I was stopped in my tracks, like Smokey Robinson, tears welling, the pit of my stomach churning, when I came across Candace Hill-Montgomery's installation at New York's *Art on the Beach*. On the sands approaching the Hudson River in the middle of virtually nothing stood throngs of refrigerators, different models, years, some vintage, some right out of anybody's kitchen, filled with collard greens and not one more thing. Not even doors afforded the "owners" privacy, dignity, or a menu option. There were some greens, that's all. Fatback, hog maws, bacon, or smoked turkey wings were not available to these hungry folks, whoever they were, wherever they were. All we got to eat this day was some unseasoned greens with nary a stove in sight.

I thought about our children, I remembered our grandmother's tending mustards and collards just beyond cracked cement. I thought about slavery. We came here hungry, trying to fill our souls and stomachs with anythin'll sustain us ever since. I heard the deacons and deaconesses in spotless white strolling the rows of pews in any church not chosen to burn in these terrible times, and I saw the baskets being passed for those in need; heard the pastor mumble "Jesus wept." Knew again our task in the New World was to fill our horn with plenty, speak Ben Webster, Col-

trane, and David Murray. To make manna out the air, to survive.
That takes food.

I'm drawn to visions of Africans, like me, during the Middle
Passage. I want to know what we yearned for, dreamt of, talked
about, if we could manage. But then there is the problem of who
could we talk to or with, since we came from so many varied re-
gions of the continent, a plethora of tongues forced into some
pidgin dialect to dispel the possibilities that this experience of
slavery, indeed, erased our human abilities/needs to communi-
cate: to share a meal.

We can extrapolate the Middle Passage to the daily sojourns
of homeless families in Washington, D.C., or Portland. We can
even be more concrete and dwell on the experiences of the Haitian boat people, whose rafts, small fishing vessels, carried more
black folks away from home to forcible detention. What did /
do they bring with them on these desperate jaunts toward North
America? Is it the stuff of dried meats, putrid drinking water,
and filth that the Middle Passage cargo endured? Or is the
"plenty" that sustains these political refugees, food of a differ-
ing nature?

In "Mississippi Gulag" by Keith Antar Mason, Prince of the
Hittite Empire, the black male performance company featured
at the Brooklyn Academy of Music and Lincoln Center's Serious Fun Festival, a character by the name of Azaka reveals to us
on his trip toward Florida an amazing perception of our realities,
of what we need to survive.

> I am coming here to find you. I got plenty of fresh water and
> food. I'll make it. Then I will walk right up and say hello and
> give you back the cheap radio that fell from the sky. And you will
> know my voice. And I will spit in your privileged face. Do not be
> upset . . . We were free when you were still in chains. We never

stopping worshipping our gods. The *loa* [deity] still come to us. I
got to get you right. Privileged little boy, who can feel the anger
of the earth. You deny too much of your pain . . . you avoid my
face. Look at me, Black life has value.[1]

Amen.

These perusals of history, literature, vernacular, culture, and
philosophy, 'long with absolutely fabulous receipts (Charles-
tonian for recipes), are meant to open our hearts and minds to
what it means for black folks in the Western Hemisphere to be
full.

ENJOY IN PEACE,
NTOZAKE SHANGE
OLDE CITY, FILADELPHIA
MAY 18, 1997

CHAPTER I

What'd You People Call That?

Once again, she held the box of cookies in front of me. I took another cookie but she kept the box there, in the same place. I took yet another cookie, and another until the whole box disappeared. "Can you read what it says there?" she asked, pointing at a line of red letters. "I cannot read American," I said.

EDWIDGE DANTICAT,
"The Missing Piece,"
Krik? Krak!

THIS PARTICULAR CHILD who ate all the cookies is a character in one of Edwidge Danticat's amazing stories of life in contemporary Haiti and the Haiti of Brooklyn and Miami. Whether we speak or read American, we've had a terrible time taking freely from the table of bounty freedom's afforded the other Americans. I often wonder if the move to monolingualize this country is a push for the homogeneity of our foods as well. Once we read American will we cease to recognize ourselves, our delicacies and midnight treats?

There are moments in our past when I have to wonder how did we celebrate, why, with whom? Not Christmas or Easter or Caledonia's birthday so much as the first night north of the Mason-Dixon line before Sherman's March, or dry pants and shoes at a clean table in the Rio Grande Valley, having outwitted the border patrol at La Frontera. When we are illicit, what can we keep down, what do we offer the spirits, the trickster, *el coyote*, who led us from bondage to a liberty so tenuous we sometimes hide for years our right to be?

Frederick Douglass, the great abolitionist, was reluctant to celebrate the Fourth of July, so we can assume that his famous Fifth of July speech was not followed by racks of barbecued ribs and potato salad. Actually, long before Douglass's disillusion with Independence Day, African-Americans in Philadelphia, the Cradle of Liberty, were wrestling with authorities over who was free to do what. Why would they want to celebrate the American Declaration of Liberation while the Fugitive Slave Act, which allowed the kidnapping of free slaves back to slave states on the word of any white man, was in effect? In Gary B. Nash's *Forging Freedom* we learn:

> While white abolitionists were withdrawing to the shadows free blacks in Philadelphia continued their political campaign to abolish slavery at both state and national levels, to revoke The Fugitive Slave Act, and to obtain legislation curbing the kidnapping of free blacks . . . Beginning in 1808, when Congress finally prohibited the slave trade, Absalom Jones and other black preachers began delivering annual thanksgiving sermons on New Year's Day, the date of the prohibition of trade and also the date of Haitian independence in 1804. The appropriation of New Year's Day as the black Fourth of July seems to have started simultaneously in Jones' African Episcopal Church and in New York's African Zion Church.[1]

And so, black-eyed peas and rice or "Hoppin' John," even collard greens and pig's feet, are not so much arbitrary predilections of the "nigra" as they are symbolic defiance; we shall cele-

{6}

brate ourselves on a day of our choosing in honor of those events
and souls who are an honor to us. Yes, we eat potato salad on
Independence Day, but a shortage of potatoes up and down
Brooklyn's Nostrand Avenue in July will not create the serious
consternation and sadness I saw/experienced one New Year's
Eve, when there weren't no chitlins to be found.

Like most American families strewn far and near 'cross the
mainland, many African-American families, like my own, experience trans–cross Caribbean or Pan-American Highway isolation blues during global/national holidays. One Christmas
and New Year's my parents and siblings were somewhere 'tween
Trinidad, Santo Domingo, and Los Angeles. My daughter and
I were lucky enough to have a highly evolved horizontal family,
that is, friends and associates from different bloodlines, but of
the same spirit, reliable, loving, and alone, too, except for us.

Anyway, this one winter I was determined that Savannah, my
child, should have a typical Owens/Williams holiday, even
though I was not a gaggle of aunts and uncles, cousins, second
and third cousins twice removed, or even relatives from Oklahoma or Carolina. I was just me, Mommy, in one body and with
many memories of not enough room for all the toddlers at the tables. How could I re-create the smells of okra and rice, Hoppin'
John, baked ham, pig's feet, chitlins, collard greens, and corn
bread with syrup if I was goin'ta feed two people? Well, actually
one and a half people. She woulda counted as a half in the census.
But how we are counted in the census is enough to give me a mi-
graine, and I am trying to recount how I tried to make again my
very colored childhood and my very "black" adolescence.

So in all of Clinton-Washington where I could walk with my
shopping cart (I am truly an urban soul), there were no chitlins
or pig's feet. I remember standing with a very cold little girl right

at the mouth of the C train entrance. Were we going on a quest at dusk on New Year's Eve or were we going to be improvisationally nimble and work something out? I was cold, too, and time was not insignificant. Everything I had to prepare before midnight was goin'ta take all night. Back we went into a small market, sawdust on the floor, and a zillion island accents pushing my requests up toward the ceiling. "A pound and a half of pig tails," I say. Savannah murmured "pig tails" like I'd said Darth Vader was her biological father.

Nevertheless, I left outta there with my pig's tails, my sweet potatoes, collards, cornmeal, rice and peas, a coconut, habañera peppers, olive oil, smoked turkey wings, okra, tomatoes, corn on the cob, and some day-old bread. We stopped briefly at a liquor store for some bourbon or brandy, I don't remember which. All this so a five-year-old colored child, whose mother was obsessed with the cohesion of her childhood, could pass this on to a little girl, who was falling asleep at the dill pickle barrel, 'midst all Mama's tales about suckin' 'em in the heat of the day and sharin' one pickle with anyone I jumped double Dutch with in St. Louis.

Our biggest obstacle was yet to be tackled, though. The members of our horizontal family we were visiting, thanks to the spirits and the Almighty, were practicing Moslems. Clearly, half of what I had to make was profane, if not blasphemous in the eyes/presence of Allah. What was Elegua, Santeria's trickster spirit, goin'ta do to assist me? Or, would I have to get real colloquial and call on Brer Rabbit or Brer Fox?

As fate would have it, my friends agreed that so long as I kept the windows open and destroyed all utensils and dishes I used for these requisite "homestyle" offerings, it was a go. I'll never forget how cold that kitchen was, nor how quickly my child fell

{8}

asleep, so that I alone tended the greens, pig's tails, and corn bread. Though I ate alone that New Year's Eve, I knew a calm I must attribute to the satisfaction of my ancestors. I tried to feed us.

Obviously, the tails have gotta be washed off, even though the fat seems to reappear endlessly. When they are pink enough to suit you, put them in a large pot full of water. Turn the heat high, get 'em boilin'. Add chopped onion, garlic, and I always use some brown sugar, molasses, or syrup. Not everybody does. Some folks like their pig extremities bitter, others, like me, want 'em sweet. It's up to you. Use a large spoon with a bunch of small holes to scrape off the grayish fats that will cover your tails. You don't need this. Throw it out. Let the tails simmer till the meat falls easily from the bones. Like pig's feet, the bones are soft and suckable, too. Don't forget salt, pepper, vinegar, and any kinda hot sauce when servin' your tails. There's nothin' wrong with puttin' a heap of tails, feet, or pig's ears right next to a good-sized portion of Hoppin' John, either. Somethin' about the two dishes mix on the palate well.

Pig's Tails by Instinct

Really, we should have soaked our peas overnight, but no such luck. The alternative is to boil 'em for at least an hour after cleaning them and gettin' rid of runty, funny-lookin' portions of peas. Once again, clear off the grayish foam that's goin'ta rise to the top of your pot. Once the peas look like they are about to swell or split open, empty the water, get half as much long grain rice as peas, mix 'em together, cover with water (two knuckles'

Hoppin' John (Black-eyed Peas and Rice)

deep of female hand). Bring to a boil, then simmer. Now, you can settle for salt and pepper. Or you can be adventurous, get yourself a hammer and split open the coconut we bought and either add the milk or the flesh or both to your peas and rice. Habañera peppers chopped really finely, 'long with green pepper and onion diced ever so neatly. Is it necessary to sauté your on-ion, garlic, pepper, and such before adding to your peas and rice? Not absolutely. You can get away without all that. Simmer in your heavy kettle with the top on till the water is gone away. You want your peas and rice to be relatively firm. However, there is another school of cookin' that doesn't mix the peas with the rice until they are on the actual plate, in which case the peas have a more fluid quality and the rice is just plain rice. Either way, you've got yourself some Hoppin' John that's certain to bring you good luck and health in the New Year. Yes, mostly West Indians add the coconut, but that probably only upset Charlestonians. Don't take that to heart. Cook your peas and rice to your own likin'.

Collard Greens to Bring You Money

Wash 2 large bunches of greens carefully 'cause even to this day in winter critters can hide up in those great green leaves that're goin'ta taste so very good. If you are an anal type, go ahead and wash the greens with suds (a small squirt of dish detergent) and warm water. Rinse thoroughly. Otherwise, an individual leaf check under cold runnin' water should do. Some folks like their greens chopped just so, like rows of a field. If that's the case with you, now is the time to get your best knife out, tuck your thumb under your fingers, and go to town. On the other hand, some just want to tear the leaves up with gleeful abandon. There's nothing

*wrong with that, either. Add to your greens that are covered
with water either ¼ pound salt pork, bacon, ham hocks, 2–3
smoked turkey wings, 3–4 tablespoons olive oil, canola oil, and
the juice of 1 whole lemon, depending on your spiritual proclivi-
ties and prohibitions. Bring to a boil, turn down. Let 'em simmer
till the greens are the texture you want. Nouveau cuisine greens
eaters will have much more sculpted-looking leaves than old-
fashioned greens eaters who want the stalks to melt in their
mouths along with the leaf of the collard. Again, I add ⅓ cup
syrup, or 2 tablespoons honey, or 3 tablespoons molasses to my
greens, but you don't have to. My mother thinks I ruin my
greens that way, but she can always make her own, you know.
Serve with vinegar, salt and pepper, and hot sauce to taste.
Serves 6–8.*

*I was taught to prepare chitlins by my third and fourth cousins
on my mother's side, who lived, of course, in Texas. My father,
whose people were Canadian and did not eat chitlins at all, told
me my daughter's French-fried Chitlin taste like lobster. Most
of the time you spend making these 5 pounds of highfalutin chitlins will be spent cleaning them (even if you bought them "pre-
cleaned," remember, the butcher doesn't have to eat them!). You
need to scrub, rinse, scrub some more, turn them inside out, and
scrub even more. By the time you finish, the pile of guts in front
of you will be darn near white and shouldn't really smell at all.
Now you are ready to start the fun part. Slice the chitlins into ½-
inch strips and set them aside. Prepare a thin batter with ½ cup
flour, ½ cup milk, ⅓ bottle of beer—drink the rest—and seasonings to taste (if you forget the cayenne, may God have mercy*

*French-fried
Chitlins*

on your soul!). Heat 2–3 inches of oil or bacon grease—use what you like as long as you don't use oil that has been used to fry fish—until very hot but not burning (360–375 degrees). Dip each strip into the batter, let excess drip down, and fry until golden brown. Only fry one layer at a time and be sure to move the chitlins around in the pot. After patting away excess grease with a paper towel, serve with dirty rice, greens, and corn bread. Or you can just eat them by themselves on a roll like a po' boy.

But seriously, and here I ask for a moment of quiet meditation, what did L'Ouverture, Pétion, and Dessalines share for their victory dinner, realizing they were the first African nation, slave-free, in the New World? What did Bolivar crave as independence from Spain became evident? What was the last meal of the defiant Inca Atahualpa before the Spaniards made a public spectacle of his defeat? I only ask these questions because the *New York Times* and the *Washington Post* religiously announce the menu of every Inauguration dinner at the White House every four years. Yet I must imagine, along with the surrealistic folk artists of Le Soleil in Port-au-Prince in their depictions of L'Ouverture's triumph, what a free people chose to celebrate victory. What sated the appetites of slaves no longer slaves, Africans now Haitians, ordinary men made mystical by wont of their taste for freedom? How did we consecrate our newfound liberty? Now this may only be important to me, but it is. It is very important. I need to know how we celebrate our victories, our very survival. What did we want for dinner? What was good enough to commemorate our humanity? We know Haitians are still hungry. Don't we?

I wake each morning to a canvas by Paul Théaud of a woman, with no body as we understand a human form, walking in a lime green ocean; she is strolling by a lovely, living coral fish. But there on the shore is a young boy whose stomach is missing, simply not there. His face is scrambled with confusion. There is a fish alive, a woman with no body walking in the sea, and he is on shore with no tummy. What does it mean? Maybe Bob Marley can answer us, so we don't spend years in a daze thinking Dred Scott has transmogrified: "Dem belly full, but dey hungry/A hungry man is a angry man."

No one told me that to be dangerous one had to be ugly as well. No one told me I had to speak American to know tenderness. Speaking American ain't necessarily nourishing. I want to know what Grenada's Socialist prime minister, Maurice Bishop, had for his last meal before the tiny island's dreams were dashed by American forces in a matter of minutes. Was there anything for him to eat? Is the Haitian woman without a body heading toward New Orleans where the slave ships useta land or is she on her way to Guantanamo Bay, or maybe your back door?

CHAPTER 2

What We Don't Say in Public

the cathedral
and that small restaurant
where a friend
found us hand in hand
and passed without saying
anything that would make us
suspect that he knew
or even imagined

NICÓLAS GUILLÉN,
"In Some Springtime Place: Elegy,"
New York Love Poetry

WHEN I WAS ELEVEN in St. Louis I crouched with my daddy by the short wave radio, listening as Fidel rode triumphantly into La Habana. I did not imagine that one day I would sit in a small restaurant in La Habana Vieja with a Sandinista, romantically dining in the midst of a block-ade, no passport, no language skills, merely passion, aroma, and ideals between us. I didn't know that my child, Savannah, would be one of Cuba's Young Pioneers at Varadero Beach with the children from Zimbabwe, South Africa, Palestine, Guate-mala, and Nicaragua, sharing breakfast duty and customs: recipes. "Mommy, I made your pancakes for two hundred kids. And, Mommy, I showed 'em how to do the butt dance."

I didn't imagine running from a newly renovated old movie house desperate to escape a performance in blackface by a seemingly ancient Afro-Cuban who moved so smoothly, turning himself and his panther while balanced on only one leg, that I knew I was witness to true black magic. I recognized this man, this movement wizard, from many black and white American films, when Cuba was in vogue. Katherine Dunham vied with Carmen Miranda for favorite exotic. Grease made him shine like fresh asphalt. This dancer, who could have humbled Fred Astaire, made me ashamed. Little did I know that, old as he was, he insisted on working: doing what he knew how to do. From the beginning he had supported the Revolution, its passionate rejection of racism and poverty. What was a little blackface to him? But I couldn't grasp it. All I saw/felt was an affront to *my* idea of La Revolución, *my* idea of my beloved La Habana Vieja, which did not include burnt cork on the faces of black people in the twentieth century. I wanted to run back to America, stepping over the Florida Keys, to the mainland where I knew random jocular racism as a "harmless part of the culture." Drinking sangria, munching on some of the most beautiful avocados and oranges I've ever seen.

There under the thatched roof of this crowded open-air "adult" amusement center, I calmed down. Two compañeros, one Cuban, one Argentinean, found me with a beer in hand, avocado under tongue, dancing the night away, dancing the fear of the past into the sea. I'd never eaten a big avocado slice and downed it with a beer before, but every time I do now, I remind myself that history, our history, mustn't scare me. Our history is the stuff that rumbas are made of, mambos, the jitterbug. All of

which goes to show that our people could fly as the saying de-
clares, I didn't haveta run back to Florida after all.

Not unlike North American colonies, for many decades of
the sixteenth and seventeenth centuries, Africans outnumbered
European colonists as much as three- or fourfold in some areas,
particularly Charleston, La Habana, Belém, Salvador, and New
Orleans. These major slave trading port cities lent/sold us to one
another like so many bales of cotton or pounds of sugar. In fact,
Cuba's African population was even more isolated than we as
North Americans assume, because the importation of female
Africans was discouraged there. It is not improbable that significant male bonding evolved which we associate with doo-
wop singers on street corners in the fifties or multigenerational
gang affiliations, like the Crips or Zulu Nation. Perhaps this
bonding prepared the Western Provinces, Oriente in particular,
to fight effectively for freedom in the nineteenth century and for
the Revolution under "El Lider Fidel" in the 1950s. Without
these historical coincidences of African isolation and cultural fe-
cundity, the history of Cuba would be astoundingly different.

What I'm getting at is, How'd all these hardworking—cut-
ting cane is torturous labor—Africans get fed and what'd they
eat? The men lived in compounds not unlike the hostels we're
familiar with in pre-free Mandela apartheid, a country which
was also under a blockade. There was no way to store perishable
items, so salt curing was quite common. The equivalent of an
American snake house on any reputable plantation, *la carniceria*
was a building or room where meats were stored, salted, and,
like *bacalao* (codfish), could be used after soaking as if they
were fresh. Even though we were kept from reproducing ourselves as Africans, we somehow managed to reproduce ourselves
as mixed-blood Cubans from very early on. Our skills as trades-

men, craftsmen, and tailors bought/brought many privileges, as did our varied complexions, assuring that more than African blood ran in our veins.

There is still in La Habana Vieja a small restaurant that seats, maybe, sixteen to twenty in the cavernous ambience of a contemporary Parisian boîte. There we, I mean all of us, could mingle. As the spiritual suggests, "We could walk together, chillun/ Talk together, chillun." Perhaps in La Habana Vieja of the seventeenth century we could eat together as well.

Aporreado de Tasajo (Salt-dried Beef Stew)

Although the aporreado *I enjoyed was made from salt-dried horse meat, I'm sure the beef version is just as satisfying. Be sure to soak your 3 pounds of beef in water. Twenty-four hours is not a bad length of time. Then, brown it very quickly in 3 table-spoons olive oil. Lift it out and let your meat simmer in some boiling water that just covers it until tender. While that's going on, sauté ½ cup medium red onions, 2 cloves garlic, 2 large bell peppers finely chopped, 5–6 slices of pimento, ½ cup diced ol-ives (green or black), for approximately 5 minutes or so. Add, to taste, some sherry, oregano, and finally 4–5 sliced, peeled toma-toes. We don't want the tomatoes to lose all their shape, you see. Take your beef out of the water, but save some of the stock, about 2 cups. Now cut the beef in 2-inch chunks, shred it (do not sub-stitute ground meat, as Americans sometimes do in enchiladas). Combine the tomatoes and other vegetables with the beef and the beef stock and let simmer around a half hour. Serve over white rice or, for a real kick, over vermicelli. Not just 'cause I like him, but 'cause if it's true, now is the time to paraphrase Joe Cuba himself: "You'll like it like that."*

CHAPTER 3

All It Took Was a Road /
Surprises of Urban Renewal

*From the very start, black music authorized a private au-
tonomous, free, and even rebellious rhythm on the part of
the listener or dancer, instead of subjecting him or her to a
dominant, foreseeable, or prewritten pattern.*

CARLOS FUENTES,
The Buried Mirror

BETWEEN MANAGUA and Bluefields there are many,
many mountains. Until the short-lived victory of the
Sandinistas in 1981, there was no road. So Nicaragua was
a fairly schizophrenic little country with the black people on one
side of the mountain and the mestizos and blancos on the other,
while Amerindians made a way for themselves in the jungles as
best they could. It was very important that there be no connection between the East and West Coast populations. That way
myths and distance could weaken any resistance to the reign of
the dictator Somoza, if the threat of being "disappeared" was
insufficient. When the freeways came through our communities,
the African-American ones, my home was disappeared along
with thousands of others. We were left with no business districts,
no access to each other; what was one neighborhood was now

ten, who lived next door was now a threatening six or eight high-way lanes away, if there at all. Particularly hurt were the restau-rants and theaters where a community shares food and celebrates itself. This we already know is a deathblow to our culture, ex-troverted, raucous, and spontaneous.

Anyway, I was in Nicaragua traveling to the house in which Nicaragua's revered poet Rubén Dario was born and raised be-fore his sojourn to Europe. Here, a black North American com-ing from Managua going vaguely in the direction of the Atlantic coast, where people like me lived, would eventually see me, too. I was anxious, divining this reunion of another lost portion of the Diaspora. This anxiety didn't last long, however, for no sooner had I begun to be acutely aware of my "racial" difference from everyone around me (poets though they were, like me, in a na-tion of poets), than someone's radio blasted Willie Colón and Celia Cruz singing "Usted Abuso." The bus rang out with every imaginable accented Spanish singing, all swaying to my *salsero preferido* (favorite salsa singer). The South Bronx had survived and pulled a trick on the Major Deegan. The blockade against Cuba lacked a sense of rhythm. But it didn't stop there. Next came Stevie Wonder and Michael Jackson rockin' our lit-tle bus through a war-torn, earthquake-ravaged land. The tales of our people's incompetency and addiction to failure must be very bad jokes indeed.

Even more important was running into Nicaraguan poet Car-los Johnson. He reminded me of a painter friend of mine from Nashville, except for the West Indian tinge to his English. At the front porch of his house, Rubén Dario met us with a poem. Then came many poems from me, that to this very day stem from that moment of underestimating who and what I come from.

"My Song for Hector Lavoe"

Mira / tu puedes ir conmigo /
hasta managua and / the earthquake was no more a surprise /
than you / con su voz / que viene de los dioses / and the
swivel of hips de su flaca / as you dance or / when she
sucks the hearts / out of the eggs of / tortugas / anglos die to
see float about / while all the time we dance around
them / split up / change
partners and fall madly in love . . . porque
nosotros somos an army of marathon dancers / lovers / seekers
and / we have never met an enemy we can't outlive.[1]

It turned out that Carlos used the racismo of the ruling class to his own advantage by wandering "aimlessly" around Managua as if he were an itinerant musician, like all black people, saxophone case in hand. Only this poet's musical instrument was an AK-47, which was used strategically to undermine the Somoza regime and lead to what we nostalgically now call La Victoria. I heard this story and others like it once we'd made it back to Managua, full of deep, sweet black rum, black music, and relentless appetites.

In what we could call a tropical ice house, a dance hall under a thatched roof, open to the night air and the call of romance, we dance to something called Nicason, a *mezcla* (mixture) of reggae, beguine, and cumbé with a ranchero overlay. You see, road or no road, we connect to the culture of the people we live with, whether they like us or not, or even if they've never seen one of us: they know James Brown. In the sweat and swivel of dancing, being hungry for more of life, and each other, we ate *huevos de tortugas*, everybody.

Turtle Eggs and Spices   *This is very simple to prepare because there is nothing to cook. Gather some young turtle eggs (substitute quail eggs where necessary). Lay them on a bed of fresh, clean, dry lettuce, spinach, arugula, it's up to you. Place 4–6 eggs on the greens. Pierce the top of the eggs gently so that the whole egg doesn't crack—we don't want that. Make your presentation as extravagant or simple as you choose, placing edible flowers, orange or lemon peels, fruits or dried fish, in an attractive manner about the eggs. In another area prepare small dishes of crushed nuts, pico de gallo (a mixture of tomatoes, peppers, onion, garlic, and cilantro), peppers, pimiento, chopped olives, fish roe, and so forth, to be placed in the small holes we've made in the eggs by our guests who will leisurely "suck the hearts and spices" out of the eggs at their whim. This is a very sexy little dish. Sits well on the tummy, lightly, so to speak, so that dancing and romancing can continue without mitigation. (Please be aware that raw eggs may contain salmonella bacteria.)*

That night in Managua we were able to cover the scars of war with poetry, music, and abandon ourselves to the impulses of our bodies in the night heat and each other's arms. The volcano where Somoza dropped the bodies of anyone for any reason was covered with mist and clouds. I only thought once about the house I grew up in that had disappeared and been resurrected as a police station. The thought broke my heart, but the fact of all of us let me hold my head high.

CHAPTER 4

Birthday in Brixton

THE BASIL RATHBONE black-and-white classic films
of London in a terrific fog, moisture enough to have curled
the hair of the wife of Frankenstein (as played by Elsa
Lanchester) without electricity are true. But when the sun comes
out in Brixton, a heavily West Indian working-class neighborhood, all kinda miracles come about. Colors challenging visions
dulled by winter's mists and rains dance up and down Railton
Road like so many butterflies come out they cocoons. It was on
such a day, when the heat reminded everyone of home, Saint
Kitts, Jamaica, Barbados, Ghana, Nigeria, Egypt, Trinidad, Sri
Lanka, wherever the sun had refused to set before she fell into
our laps, a free fire of possibility, our folks paraded themselves in
strolls particular to their pre-London homes round and through
the Brixton market.

I say this only to say that shopping in Brixton is as much fun as
shopping in Texas's Fiesta markets, *Nuestros Cachitos* (our little
stores). Our music from Yellow Man to Youssour N'Dour blar-
ing from vegetable stands proffering tubers of every size and
color, peppers whose scent from a distance brings tears to the
eyes, and midriffs sportin' more of us at the nipple, on the infant
bottle, suckin' no different than the palm wine drinkard's
wildest dreams, if we take Amos Tutola at his word.

My daughter and I were looking for a typical special dinner

{23}

from the Americas, if such a thing is possible. I had to shop for a very good friend's surprise birthday party on Mayal Road down from Marcus Garvey Square. We found, amazingly, sweet looking carrots, fresh red beans (kidney beans), paratha (an East Indian flatbread) straight from the loving hands of the wife of the *halal* butcher. Now a *halal* butcher is the Moslem equivalent of a kosher butcher. In other words, the meats and poultry are slaughtered in a specific way and then blessed by an imam before being suitable for consumption.

Savannah and I found a miraculous rack of lamb that did not stretch our budget too very much. We also picked fresh watercress and cucumber and beets for a salad to be graced with rosemary and mayonnaise. I had a vague recollection of *niddah*, an Orthodox Jewish practice of women bathing in reverence and humility at a certain time during the Hebrew calendar. After consulting with my spirit guides and my daughter, I decided that we should do our best to prepare a special bath for our friend and hostess, Leila, who was certain this day that she was at the nadir of her life as a woman, an exile, a wog who should go back where she came from, which would simply mean that she would come here, to the New World, where all of us whose history is disrupted by the slave trade belong.

Well, we covered every inch of the house on Mayal Street, the house where C. L. R. James, the father of the West Indian democratic movement, was so loved and respected during his lifetime, with flowers and vines and incense, never allowing the smoldering hints of C. L. R.'s presence to be overshadowed. Once I believed I could hear him muttering: "Enough child, enough. You've made your point now." But we weren't done until we had filled Leila's tub with drops of rose water, Florida water, and so many roses, African daisies, violets, aranda orchids, carnations, and lavender that we could hardly imagine how her ample body was going to fit.

Though C. L. R. James's head was a tousled nappy mess of ivory cotton, rivaling a good German Saint Nick, I hoped he was tending the door to the bath so that Leila's giggles of pleasure and surprise would not end before we'd finished preparing her birthday supper. I am sure even in his nineties C. L. R. would have assisted us. He had a weakness for bright women, especially when he could say he was a part of giving them something wonderful.

We broiled most of Leila's repast in the garden on a regular grill with charcoal seasoned with tequila and lavender. We basted the rack of lamb with olive oil and salt and pepper. Between the fat on the outside of the cut of meat and the meat itself, we inserted minced garlic and rosemary. Then we simply laid the meat on the grill (coals are gray-red) till we decided it was ready. We had some problems here because everybody's rare is not the same and well done might as well be burnt to a crisp to others. Luckily we were all friends, still are. We also made red beans and rice, which we make the same way we make black-eyed peas and rice. The paratha we turned over and over on the grill, like American flapjacks or pizza to get the outside honey brown. Alu paratha has a mixture of potatoes and herbs as fillings and should not be flung about so cavalierly. There was mango ice cream for dessert. Unfortunately, none of the flowers Savannah and I were able to find for Leila were edible.

Leila's Birthday Surprise Supper / She Really Didn't Know— Rack of Lamb

Oh, I almost forgot. One reason I turn so frequently to East Indian or Moslem references is that Trinidad and Tobago, where
Leila's life partner, Darcus Howe, and some of my people hail
from, is either one-half or two-thirds (depends on whom you
talk to) East Indian. Guess why this is the case in Guyana, Suriname, and Trinidad. Right! Somebody had to work those rice
paddies. Only by the late nineteenth century slavery was illegal, indentured servitude was not. Sound familiar? Check your
James Fenimore Cooper. Or if you find it more in the spirit of
things, C. L. R. James's own *The Black Jacobins*: "Now we are
independent. We own the soil. We have our own name. We have
our flag. Let us have some wine and some music."[1]

CHAPTER 5

Too Many Fish in the Sea

"Where was your mind was whole night?"
"Africa."

"Oh? You walk?"
The mate held up his T-shirt, mainly a red hole,
and wriggled it on. He tested the bamboo pole
that trawled the skipping lure from the fast-shearing hull
with the Trade behind them.

"Mackerel running," he said.
"Africa, right! You get sunstroke, chief. That is all."

DEREK WALCOTT,
Omeros

MACKEREL MAY HAVE BEEN runnin' that bright sunlit day, but it was not mackerel folks was runnin' they mouths 'bout, that spring Brian Lara led the West Indians to trounce the United Kingdom, legendary cricke-teer Gary Sobers was knighted, and David Rudder of Antigua led a whole stadium of island hoppin' Caribbeans, like true bal-ladeers, in singing: "It's a pan man's war, yes me brodah." While the rest of the Caribbean concerned itself with play and work, Trinidadians and Barbadians prepared to go to The Hague and the World Court about the matter of the flyin' fish.

It seems that the Trinidad and Tobago fishermen were plyin' the seas beyond their legal boundaries, catchin' up all the flyin' fish so essential to a Barbadian diet. This is a wee bit of a fish we are now discussin', by the way, with a sweet, tender taste to it (so long as the sack of poison it carries is removed before cookin'). The whole of the Caribbean News Service, Barbados TV, and Trinidad and Tobago Television were steeped in scores of cricket matches and interviews with the man on the island street's opinion of the flyin' fish situation.

While Barbadians consume the fish, Trinidadians do not. It was, therefore, an ugly and greedy act on the part of the Trinidad and Tobago fishermen to set their nets out for a fish they don't eat, in waters that aren't their own waters, to sell it back to Barbadians from Barbadian waters with the price reachin' half to the moon. The other side of the argument was if the Barbadians wanted the flyin' fish so much, why didn't they roll up their sleeves and catch them for themselves? Trinidadian fishermen were only answering the demands of the market; they didn't even eat the creature. That was what was so galling to the Barbadians. Trinidadians don't even want the fish, but they chasin' flyin' fish through the sea like it was they mothers' last dyin' request. Trinidadians simply reply, "We catch the fish so we can sell it to you." "Back to us, you mean." Barbadians seethe. "Oh, but you not we only customer, ya see," I can hear a seaman from La Fillette reply. "Dem Japanese want some of we catch as well, now." And so it goes on and on, the aggressive, mercantile Trinidad and Tobago fishermen, no doubt supported by their government, stealing and selling, at loan-shark rates, the poor flyin' fish back to those who truly appreciate its delicate flavor. The matter has yet to be adjudicated at The Hague, but it's on the Court's docket.

If we were to find our kitchen a-run with flyin' fish, we must remember to *take the poison out*. Then, floured or not, fried or broiled, do it quickly in hot oil that will not distract from the true sweetness of the meat (no peanut oil). Cookin' flyin' fish is rather like preparin' shrimp, in the sense that undercookin' is difficult while overcookin' can take place in one second's gesture to answer the phone in the next room.

Heaven only knows what kind of ruckus Trinidadians would raise if Barbadians came after their treasured shark meat, which to hear them tell it is never dry, so long as you know what you are doing in your own kitchen.

First, let your favorite fisherman know that you a-lookin' for Cousin *him to bring ya a good sturdy shark, but not too big unless you* Eddie's Shark *expectin' all the family from Port-of-Spain and San Fernando to* with *show up. See if he can't find somebody to share the shark with* Breadfruit *ya so ya don't waste the meat. Have him get one of his men to clean it for ya, they'll only be lookin' for a bit of change, ya see. Let them fillet it as well—be sure to mention that. Shark is not the easiest fish to chop up, I can tell ya that. Okay, wash it off really well. If the water has been turned off for the day, make sure you're at Lower Village Pump in time to get enough to boil 1 large breadfruit and 4–5 green bananas. Water won't come back, if it's been shut off, till after you want all your cookin' done with.*

Okay, baste your ¾–1-inch shark meat in some coconut oil and a dash of Girley's pepper sauce. Oil the grill too, so your shark don't stick, fall apart. Then, season the shark with garlic, if you choose. But don't use too many things. Set your shark on the broiler for no more than 5–6 minutes. It's not goin'ta turn all brown now, but a honey color, to my mind. Take it off the grill and cover so them safe from fly and other pest.

Now, in a large pot full of boiling water, set your green bananas (with peels) and breadfruit slices. You've peeled and seeded the breadfruit already. Don't be afraid when it changes to a blood red color, that's the mourning of our ancestors, hungry for us to live now. Okay, boil these up in your water with some cilantro, garlic, onion, and pepper to taste. When they are easily pierced by your fork, they are ready to eat. That's how I do it and me mohda before that.

CHAPTER 6

Brazil: More African
Than Africans

Brazilians' ... personal experience made it impossible to accept such a dehumanizing and absolutist system especially of racial segregation when it came to the mulatto.

THOMAS E. SKIDMORE,
The Idea of Race in Latin America

HAVING SPENT considerable time in Brazil, north and south, I can assure you that being what they see as a *prieto*, "black-black," like asphalt, or being *branca*, almost "lily white," both have salient drawbacks. The south of Brazil, industrialized and modern and mythologically white, has been populated by millions of Brazilians who, although they may not be exactly prieto, are definitely not white. To see the "Africans," I was always directed to the north, to Bahia. This was quite confusing to me, because anywhere I walked in Brazil, I saw folks who looked colored to me. Nevertheless, I sadly came to understand what my southern Brazilian acquaintances meant, when I finally did go to Bahia, just to go, but not to see the Africans, which I could do by myself in my hotel with a mirror.

Nearly twenty years ago, I asked a class of mine at university in Bahia to bring in the beginning of a performance piece or a one-act play based on their lives and world as they understood it. Every single presentation was based on a myth, albeit a real African myth, but a myth nonetheless with Ogun, Yemaya, and Babaluye raising Cain in downtown Salvador, or some unnamed mountain pass. This was alarming. My students were validating themselves as the "other" where they were not the other. I contained my frustrations as long as I could until finally I asked them to just stop for one minute. I asked, calmly as I knew how, "What would happen to all of us in Salvador if a nuclear weapon exploded? Can a nuclear weapon affect the daily life of the gods in the same way it affected the people of Hiroshima or Chernobyl?"

There was a terrible silence in our room. It's easier to hide inside a myth, as Paul Laurence Dunbar said in "We Who Wear the Mask," even at the risk of being Maya Angelou's singing caged bird. I have no recollection of the gods Xango or Oxossi's presence at the last meeting of the Organization of American States. Their absence, unlike Fidel's, was not even noted. We are not folklore. As the recent elections of African-Brazilians to the Brazilian Senate attests. The epitome and apex of Brazilian life may be the continually multiplying mulatta, but we must all eat whatever our hue, or the hue and cry over who we are.

Naturally we begin with the crux of our main dishes, which is rice. The same Guinea and Angola population so fawned over by Carolinians for their skills in rice cultivation also captured the imagination and entrepreneurial needs of Brazilian planters. They ate rice, so we have instead of Carolinian rice, Brazilian rice, which differs in a number of ways, as we shall see.

Using long grain rice, wash and carefully pick out dark spots, **Brazilian**
dead insects, et cetera. Heat oil in a skillet. Use vegetable, ca- **Rice**
nola, peanut, olive oil, margarine even, not butter. Fry about 2
cups of the rice with 1 finely sliced onion; doing this, stir gently
with a wood spoon until the mixture has a whirring sound like
a woman's many skirts. Let yourself take at least ten minutes,
cooking mixture over a low flame. Dryness is essential to rice
passing itself off as Brazilian. Then add 1 peeled, finely
chopped tomato and 2 tablespoons of tomato sauce. Add about
2 cups of boiling water. Continue to stir, but remove your pan
from the flame. Watch for popping now. When it's off the
flame, stir conservatively, once or twice, no more. Take your
pan back to the fire and bring to a boil. When boiling, cover,
lower heat. Cook nearly half an hour. Don't go stirring this
now. When the rice is done, take it off the stove, uncover, and
let whatever water left float off in the air. You can dress your
rice however you please, even making shapes out of it in molds
and such. The primary point, however, is once again that each
grain can stand separately, that is, on its own.

What are we going to put on this rice we've made so perfectly?
How about a dish I discovered while searching the islands of
Itaparica and Itapúa for Dona Flor and at least one of her husbands? Assuming we know to look for dende oil, which is so frequently used in Bahia, a rich dense oil from the palm *Elasesis*

guineensis, an African import along with the rest of us, let us begin with cuisine.

Shrimp
Carúrú

After we clean—you do, hopefully, know how to shell and clean shrimp—place 1 pound in melted butter, about 1 tablespoon, with chopped onion, parsley, green pepper, and tomato to taste. Grind, by hand or machine, ⅓ cup of dried shrimp and mix in a little bit more than 1 tablespoon of manioc meal. Grate some coconut meat and save the heavy milk. To what's left of the coconut water add 1 cup of real boiling water and set aside this thinned milk for later. Put your shrimp and a bit more than a cup of sliced okra in with the sautéing shrimp mixture. Keep over a simmer until your okra is soft but retains its shape. One second or two before you serve, add your coconut milk, that's right, the thick one, with some dende oil and serve over your rice. If you've done this right, whatever color African-American you are, you can surely get by as a real Bahiano do norde, believe me. I've done it, waiting patiently for one of Dona Flor's house or Gabriela's lovers to smell the aromas eking out of my small, wooden house on the winding stone-paved streets of Itaparica. But I was not too disturbed by the appearance of a very friendly Guadalupe man, who I hoped was looking for his incarnation of Dona Flor. Enough with fantasy, let's go back to our kitchens.

Although Brazilians are great meat eaters, usually chicken and fish are available to more people. While I was with the cast of *For Colored Girls . . .* —although we couldn't call it that or the public would think we only talkin' 'bout the blacks, at least this is what I was told—I had the opportunity to indulge in a typical northeastern, that is, Afro-Brazilian dish of *vatápà*, which can also be made from shrimp alone, or shrimp and fish in combination. To this day, I can still use what actors call sense memory, and we call daydreams, to re-create and savor.

Sauté 1 sliced onion, a handful of parsley, and peppers of your Chicken
choice, at least 2, with 4 peeled and chopped tomatoes in dende Vatápà
oil, preferably but not necessarily. Simmer the chicken in this mixture, adding water as needed. Our chicken is cleaned and separated at the joints and we'll let it simmer until the meat falls off the bone just as if we were preparing a Carolinian fricassee. Then we take the chicken out and cleanly, like a gangster in Detroit, take it all off the bones. Now we've got 2 grated coconuts set aside with the thick milk. Add 6 cups of water to the coconut milk and cook softly until the coconut meat is soft. We take our ½ pound of ground dried shrimp, along with the ½ pound of ground roasted peanuts—you know you don't have to do all this by hand—and put it in the coconut milk mix. Cook for a while, add your chicken gravy. Season as you please with regular salt and pepper, then strain. If needed, thicken your brew with 1–2 tablespoons moistened rice flour. Put in the chicken and the thick coconut milk and heat very, very slowly. Your dish should have the texture of a heavy white sauce. Remove from the heat. Serve over rice or the equivalent of sweet spoon bread.

The song that made Carmen Miranda famous was "Watercolor of Brazil," which would have to include the national dish of Brazil, *feijoada*. There are a number of feijoadas, which is traditionally served with collard greens, farina, and orange peels, but I picked a feijoada I hankered after months after leaving Bahia.

Zaki's Favorite Feijoada

First we soak about 1 pound of jerked beef in cold water overnight. (We already learned how to do this.) Soak 4 cups of black beans overnight, too. Next day, drain your beef, cover with cold water, bring it to a brisk boil, and keep it there 5 minutes or so. Drain this again and let it cool down a bit. Add all your other meats, 1 pound each of smoked sausage, smoked pork, smoked tongue, some bacon, and 3 pig's feet. Bring all this to a boil slowly and simmer till the meats are tender to the prick of a fork. In your other pot, set your drained beans, cover up with cold water, and without any kind of seasoning let them boil, too, till almost tender. Drain the beans.

Put the mixtures from both pots together in one big pot; keep over a low flame until meats are very, very tender and the beans are soft enough to burst out of their skins. While this is going on, hum your favorite tune and fry 1 chopped shallot, 1 onion, chopped up too, with some spicy link sausage torn into little pieces, until everything is brown. Put in 1 cup of the cooked beans, mash it all up, then stir in a bit of bean juices and let this simmer 5 to 10 minutes.

Pull your meats out of the beans and prepare a nice presentation of them in an orderly and proportionate manner on a large platter. Traditionally the tongue is placed in the middle with the other meats 'round it. Use the bean juice as gravy over the meats. Put the beans in a large bowl with a nice rice, some orange slices, pepper and lemon sauce, or cooked farina. You may drink what you like, but cachaca *is the Brazilian equivalent of tequila. So, when in Brazil, et cetera.*

(These are posoles.*) Add 2 cups cooked, drained hominy to about 4 cups of scalded milk with 1 cup of thickened coconut milk together with 3 whole cloves, 1 cinnamon stick, 1 teaspoon salt, 1 cup sugar, and simmer for near 45 minutes. Then put in your 1 tablespoon of butter, ½ cup of crushed peanuts, 1 teaspoon of rose flower water, if you can find it, and add rice flour as needed to thicken and get a creamy texture. Serve cold with cinnamon sprinkled on top.* Brazilian Hominy (Mungunza or Chá de Burro)

Now, if this doesn't bring to mind Amado's *Gabriela, Cinnamon, and Clove,* I don't know what will. In Bahia, where the Amado family has a restaurant named after another one of Jorge's novels, *Tent of Miracles,* this dish is eaten with a spoon. A heavier, more solid type of mungunza, called *mungunza para corbar* (hominy to cut) is spooned into a dish lined with banana fronds and allowed to cool, cut in squares, and served cold. The highest concentration of folks of African descent outside the continent of Africa live and eat in Brazil. We eat what they eat, just differently. These recipes have stayed with us for centuries, being improvised here and there, where we found that somethin' we were accustomed to in, say, Guinea was not available at the mouth of the Amazon.

The same process nurtured Brazilian music, dance, and vernacular poetry, which I imagine went on not far from the campfires, fireplaces, kitchens of hungry people in festive moods. Dancing the *chorro*, the Brazilian equivalent of a Cuban *Sazón*, a *mezcla* (mixture) of European waltzes and polkas with African rhythms punctuating the melody, or bouts of *repentismo* during which poets of varied powers improvise lyrics one after the other: how we play the dozens.

If this is not sufficient to build up your appetite, we can invite you to a few playful rounds of *capoeira*, which is deadly if done with seriousness. Capoeira, a dance similar to martial arts, like some of the foods we've been discussing, is a direct import, like we were, from the coast of Angola. If basketball is likened to an athlete's ballet, then capoeira is a kick boxer's jitterbug. Barefoot, flying through the air like the Savoy dancers of the 1930s, capoeira masters are pushed by the irrepressible syncopation of the *berimbau* (a stringed instrument on an arc of wood that can be plucked or bowed), the *stabaque* (a percussion instrument), and the quirky *cuica* (a drum that varies in range and intensity with the pull of a string and the drummer's imagination). Capoeira is taken lightly, or as lifesaver by police assigned to the huge *favelas* (shanty towns) that ring Brazilian cities. Here the law can be in anybody's hands.

When my father wandered up into Rosinha in Rio, a policeman asked me where he'd gone. I pointed up to the hills. He shook his head sadly. "Why, we don't even go up there." But Daddy's inimitable street smarts and good looks apparently worked well for him. I thought maybe these are urban *quilimbos* (urban maroon settlements), where we are a law, a culture unto ourselves, but such is not the case. As Lygia Fagundes Telles reminds us in the stirring novel *The Girl in the Photograph*, Brazil endured terrible political upheavals in the mid-twentieth century, just as we in North America struggled with. The difference being that Brazil at that time was a police state.

> There they interrogated me [Bernado] for twenty-five hours, as they shouted, "Traitor to your country, traitor." Nothing was given me to eat or drink during this time. Afterwards, they carried me to the so-called chapel: the torture chamber. Then a ceremony was initiated. It was frequently repeated and took from three to six hours each session. First, they asked me if I belonged to any political group. I denied it. So they wrapped wires around my fingers, beginning the electric torture: they administered shocks to me weak at first and then becoming stronger and stronger. Next, they obliged me to strip off my clothes. I was nude and unprotected.[1]

Arbitrary violence or premeditated violence conducted by the state was integral to our first experiences in the New World. The idea that "all that's over with" is not only naive but dangerous, because we then deny the very connective tissue of our historical realities. Just consider the ravaging of the Amazon rain forest, the Crips and Bloods or beggars and huffers in São Paulo. But we have managed to survive, to live.

Africans and African-Americans who visit Brazil come away with an almost mystical attachment, which is summed up beautifully in another passage from Fagundes Telles.

> I used to think about my people, I knew I wouldn't go back but I kept on thinking about them so much. Like when you take a dress out of a trunk, a dress you're not going to wear, just to look

at it. To see what it was like. Afterwards one folds it up again and puts it away but one never considers throwing it away or giving it to anyone. I think that's what missing things is.[2]

We are blessed, since we can find our ovens and stoves and make up for some of what we long for.

CHAPTER 7

What Is It We Really Harvestin' Here?

W E GOT A SAYIN', "The blacker the berry, the
sweeter the juice," which is usually meant as a com-
pliment. To my mind, it also refers to the delectable
treats we as a people harvested for our owners and for our own
selves all these many years, slave or free. In fact, we knew something about the land, sensuality, rhythm, and ourselves that has
continued to elude our captors—puttin' aside all our treasures in
the basement of the British Museum, or the Met, for that matter.
What am I talkin' about? A different approach to the force of
gravity, to our bodies, and what we produce: a reverence for the
efforts of the group and the intimate couple. Harvest time and
Christmas were prime occasions for courtin'. A famine, a
drought, a flood, or Lent do not serve as inspiration for couplin',
you see.

The Juba, a dance of courtin' known in slave quarters of
North America and the Caribbean, is a phenomenon that stayed
with us through the jitterbug, the wobble, the butterfly, as a
means of courtin' that's apparently very colored, and very "African." In fact we still have it and we've never been so "inte-
grated"—the *Soul Train* dancers aren't all black anymore, but
the dynamic certainly is. A visitor to Cuba in Lynne Fauley Emery's *Black Dance: 1619 to Today* described the Juba as a series
of challenges.

A woman advances and commencing a slow dance, made up of shuffling of the feet and various contortions of the body, thus challenges a rival from among the men. One of these, bolder than the rest, after a while steps out, and the two then strive which shall tire the other; the woman performing many feats which the man attempts to rival, often excelling them, amid the shouts of the rest. A woman will sometimes drive two or three successive beaux from the ring, yielding her place at length to some impatient belle.[1]

John Henry went up against a locomotive, but decades before we simply were up against ourselves and the elements. And so we are performers in the fields, in the kitchens, by kilns, and for one another. Sterling Stuckey points out, in *Slave Culture*, however, that by 1794 "it was illegal to allow slaves to dance and drink on the premises . . . without the written consent of their owners," the exceptions being Christmas and the burials, which are communal experiences.[2] And what shall we plant and harvest, so that we might "Hab big times duh fus hahves, and duh fus ting wut growed we take tuh duh church so as ebrybody could hab a piece ub it. We pray over it and shout. Wen we hab a dance, we use tuh shout in a ring. We ain't have wutyuh call a propuh dance tuday."[3]

Say we've gone about our owners' business. Planted and harvested his crop of sugar cane, remembering that the "ratio of slaves/sugar was ten times that of slaves/tobacco and slaves/cotton."[4] That to plant a sugar crop we have to dig a pit three feet square and a few inches deep into which one young plant is set. Then, of course, the thing has to grow. A mature sugar-cane plant is three to nine feet tall. That's got to be cut at exactly the right point. Then we've got to crush it, boil it, refine it, from thick black syrup to fine white sugar, to make sure, as they say in

Virginia, that we "got the niggah out." Now it's time to tend to our own gardens. Let's grow some sweet potatoes to "keep the niggah alive."

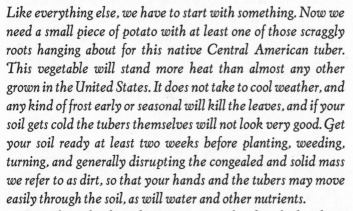

Like everything else, we have to start with something. Now we **Sweet**
need a small piece of potato with at least one of those scraggly **Potatoes**
roots hanging about for this native Central American tuber. This vegetable will stand more heat than almost any other grown in the United States. It does not take to cool weather, and any kind of frost early or seasonal will kill the leaves, and if your soil gets cold the tubers themselves will not look very good. Get your soil ready at least two weeks before planting, weeding, turning, and generally disrupting the congealed and solid mass we refer to as dirt, so that your hands and the tubers may move easily through the soil, as will water and other nutrients.

Once the soil is free of winter, two weeks after the last frost, plant the potato slips in 6–12-inch ridges, 3–4½ feet apart. Separate the plants by 9–12 inches. If we space the plants more than that, our tubers may be grand, but way too big to make good use of in the kitchen. We should harvest our sweet potatoes when the tubers are not quite ripe, but of good size, or we can wait until the vines turn yellow. Don't handle our potatoes too roughly, which could lead to bruising and decay. If a frost comes upon us unexpectedly, take those potatoes out the ground right away. Our potatoes will show marked improvement during storage, which allows the starch in them to turn to sugar. Nevertheless let them lie out in the open for 2 to 3 hours to fully dry. Then move them to a moist and warm storage space. The growing time for our crop'll vary from 95 to 125 days.

The easiest thing to do with a sweet potato is to bake it. In its skin. I coat the thing with olive oil, or butter in a pinch. Wrap it in some aluminum foil, set it in the oven at 400 degrees. Wait till I hear sizzling, anywhere from 45 minutes to an hour after, in a very hot oven. I can eat it with my supper at that point or I can let it cool off for later. (One of the sexiest dates I ever went on was to the movies to see El Mariachi. *My date brought along chilled baked sweet potatoes and ginger beer. Much nicer than canola-sprayed "buttered" popcorn with too syrupy Coca-Cola, wouldn't you say?)*

Mustard Greens

No, they are not the same as collards. We could say they, with their frilly edges and sinuous shapes, have more character, are more flirtatious, than collards. This green can be planted in the spring or the fall, so long as the soil is workable (not cold). It's not a hot weather plant, preferring short days and temperate climates. We can use the same techniques for mustard greens that we use for lettuce. Sowing the seeds in rows 12–18 inches apart, seedlings 4–8 inches apart. These plants should get lots of fertilizer to end up tender, lots of water, too. They should be harvested before they are fully mature. Now, you've got to be alert, because mustard greens grow fast, 25–40 days from the time you set them in the soil to harvest. When it comes time to reap what you've sown, gather the outer leaves when they are 3–4 inches long, tender enough; let the inner leaves then develop more or wait till it's hot and harvest the whole plant.

Now we cook the mustard greens just like the collards, or we don't have to cook it at all. This vegetable is fine in salads or on sandwiches and soups. If you shy away from pungent tastes, mix these greens with some collards, kale, or beet greens. That should take some of the kick out of them. I still like my peppers and vinegar, though. If we go back, pre-Columbus, the Caribs did, too. According to Spanish travelers, the Caribs, who fancied vegetables, added strong peppers called aji-aji to just about everything. We can still find aji-aji on some sauces from Spanish-speaking countries if we read the labels carefully. Like "La Morena." So appropriate.

The watermelon is an integral part of our actual life as much as **Watermelon** it is a feature of our stereotypical lives in the movies, posters, racial jokes, toys, and early American portraits of the "happy darky." We could just as easily been eatin' watermelon in D. W. Griffith's Birth of a Nation *as chicken legs. The implications are the same. Like the watermelon, we were a throwback to "African" pre-history, which isn't too off, since Lucy, the oldest* Homo sapiens *currently known, is from Africa, too.*

But I remember being instructed not to order watermelon in restaurants or to eat watermelon in any public places because it makes white people think poorly of us. They already did that, so I don't see what the watermelon was going to precipitate. Europeans brought watermelon with them from Africa anyway. In Massachusetts by 1629 it was recorded as "abounding." In my rebelliousness as a child, I got so angry about the status of the watermelon, I tried to grow some in the flower box on our front porch in Missouri. My harvest was minimal to say the least.

Here's how you can really grow you some watermelon. They like summer heat, particularly sultry, damp nights. If we can grow watermelons, we can grow ourselves almost any other kind of melon. *The treatment is the same. Now, these need some space, if we're looking for a refrigerator-sized melon or one ranging from 25–30 pounds. Let them have a foot between plants in between rows 4–6 feet apart. They need a lot of fertilizer, especially if the soil is heavy and doesn't drain well. When the runners (vines) are a foot to a foot and a half long, fertilize again about 8 inches from the plant itself. Put some more fertilizer when the first melons appear. Watermelons come in different varieties, but I'm telling you about the red kind. I have no primal response to a golden or blanched fleshed melon. Once your melons set on the vines and start to really take up some space, be sure not to forget to water the vines during the ripening process.*

When is your watermelon ripe? You can't tell by thumping it nor by the curly tail at the point where the melon is still on the vine. The best way to know if your melon is ready is by looking at the bottom. The center turns from a light yellow to deep amber. Your melon'll have a powdery or mushy tasteless sorta taste if you let it ripen too long.

Surely you've seen enough pictures or been to enough picnics to know how to eat a watermelon, so I won't insult you with that information. However, there is a fractious continuing debate about whether to sprinkle sugar or salt on your watermelon slice. I am not going to take sides in this matter.

Some of us were carried to the New World specifically because we knew 'bout certain crops, knew 'bout the groomin' and harvestin' of rice, for instance.

> Plantation owners were perfectly aware of the superiority . . . of African slaves from rice country. Littlefield (journalist) writes

that "as early as 1700 ships from Carolina were reported in the
Gambia River" ... In a letter dated 1756, Henry Laurens, a
Charleston merchant, wrote, "The slaves from the River Gambia are prefer'd to all others with us save the Gold Coast." The
previous year he had written: "Gold Coast or Gambias are best;
next to them the Windward Coast are prefer'd to Angolas."[5]

These bits of information throw an entirely different, more
dignified light on "colored" cuisine, for me. Particularly since I
was raised on rice and my mother's people on both sides are inde-
fatigable Carolinians, South, to be exact, South Carolinians. To
some, our "phrenologically immature brains" didn't have con-
sequence until our mastery of the cultivation of "cargo,"
"patna," "joponica," and finally Carolina rice, "small-grained,
rather long and wiry, and remarkably white" was transferred to
the books and records of our owners.[6] Nevertheless, our pen-
chant for rice was not dampened by its relationship to our bondage. Whether through force or will, we held on to our rice-eatin'
heritage. I repeat, I was raised on rice. If I was Joe Williams, insteada singin' "Every day, every day, I sing the blues," I'd be
sayin', "Oh, every day, almost any kinda way, I get my rice."

My poor mother, Eloise, Ellie, for short, made the mistake of
marrying a man who was raised by a woman from Canada. So
every day, he wanted a potato, some kinda potato, mashed,
boiled, baked, scalloped, fried, just a potato. Yet my mother was
raising a sixth generation of Carolinians, which meant we had to
eat some kinda rice. Thus, Ellie was busy fixing potato for one
and rice for all the rest every day, until I finally learnt how to do
one or the other and gave her a break. I asked Ellie Williams
how her mother, Viola, went about preparing the rice for her
"chirren"—a Low-country linguistic lapse referring to offspring like me. Anyway, this is what Mama said.

{47}

Mama's Rice "We'd buy some rice in a brown paper bag [this is in The Bronx]. Soak it in a bit of water. Rinse it off and cook it the same way we do now." "How is that, Ma?" I asked. "Well, you boil a certain amount of water. Let it boil good. Add your rice and let it boil till tender. Stirring every so often because you want the water to evaporate. You lift your pot. You can tell if your rice is okay because there's no water there. Then you fluff it with a fork. You want every kind, extra, extra, what you call it. No ordinary olive oil will do.

"Heat this up. Just a little bit of it. You don't want no greasy rice, do you? Heat this until, oh, it is so hot that the smoke is coming quick. Throw in 3–4 cloves garlic, maybe 1 cup chopped onion too, I forgot. Let that sizzle and soften with ½ cup each cilantro, pimiento, and everything. But don't let this get burned, no. So add your 4 cups water and 2 cups rice. Turn up the heat some more till there's a great boiling of rice, water, seasonings. The whole thing. Then leave it alone for a while with the cover on so all the rice cooks even. Now, when you check and see there's only a small bit of water left in the bottom of the pot, stir it all up. Turn the heat up again and wait. When there's no water left at all, at all. Just watch the steam coming up. Of course you should have a good pegau (crispy brown rice) by now, but the whole pot of your rice should be delicioso, ready even for my table. If you do as I say."

For North Americans, a pot with burnt rice on the bottom is a scary concept. But all over the Caribbean, it's a different story entirely. In order to avoid making *asopao*—a rice moist and heavy with the sofrito or tomato-achiote mixture, almost like a thick soup where the rice becomes one mass instead of standing, each grain on its own—it is necessary to let the rice at the bottom of the pot get a crustlike bottom, assuring that all moisture has evaporated. My poor North American mother, Ellie, chastises me frequently for "ruining" good rice with all this spice. Then I remind her that outside North America we Africans were left to cook in ways that reminded us of our mother's cooking, not Jane Austen's characters. The rice tastes different, too. But sometimes I cheat and simply use Goya's Sazón—after all, I'm a modern woman. I shouldn't say that too loudly, though. Mathilde can hear all the way from her front porch any blasphemous notion I have about good cooking. No, it is her good cooking that I am to learn. I think it is more than appropriate that we know something about some of the crops that led to most of us African descendants of the Diaspora, being here, to eat anything at all.

But rather than end on a sour note, I am thinking of my classes with the great Brazilian dancer, choreographer, and teacher Mercedes Baptista at the now legendary Clark Center. We learned a harvest dance, for there are many, but the movements of this celebratory ritual were lyrical and delicate, far from the tortured recounts of Euro-Americans to our "jigaboo" gatherings; no gyrations, repetitive shuffling that held no interest. Indeed, the simple movement of the arms, which we worked on for days until we got it, resembled a tropical port-de-bras worthy of any ballerina. Our hip movements, ever so subtle, with four switches to the left, then four to the right, all the while turning and covering space. The head leaning in the direction of the hips, the arms moving against it, till the next hip demanded counterpoint.

A healthy respect for the land, for what we produce for the blessing of a harvest begot dances of communal joy. On New Year's Eve in the late fifties, we danced the Madison; today it's a burning rendition of "The Electric Slide." Eighty-year-olds jammin' with toddlers after the weddin' toast. No, we haven't changed so much.

CHAPTER 8

Westward Ho! Anywhere Must Be Better'n Here!

THERE WERE definitive problems even in the settling and exploration of the wild, wild western territories, where all things were possible so long as neither the taint of slavery nor the constancy of African blood reminded anyone of the fact of one's blackness. Even the aromas of the food we were probably preparing for someone of a "higher" station was sneered at and debased. But like all good cooks, I've no doubt that we carried along home (urban slaves had much greater freedom of mobility than their rural, plantation-bound brethren), a carcass or two that could rise to the occasion of a decent stew or bit of broth for a vegetable entrée. The aroma of a chicken, leg of lamb, venison shank, beef ribs, pheasant legs, was the smell of our mother's love and imagination. It's easy enough to envision.

Surely runaway slaves, Africans assimilated by Chippewa, Lumpi, Cherokee, Seminole, or Navajo, were familiar with dishes such as these. Since whether we were welcomed to the western territories or not, we had to eat. It was illegal for us to carry firearms in all slave states and some northern ones, but in the western territories, somehow, somebody forgot to let us know that to arm ourselves was an act worthy of hanging. Maybe by arming ourselves we protected ourselves from hanging.

And as living human beings, I'm sure we were amazed and

jumbled by the bounty of meats and vegetables just waiting to sit on our tables, by our campfires, on our woodstoves, from Kansas to Oregon. Now, that is not to say we were welcome, but we had to live and we had to be free: and if we didn't follow Benjamin J. "Pap" Singleton from various points along the Mississippi to Kansas, bloody Kansas, we could hook our horses to wagons leading other restless, desperate freemen, runaways, and the manumitted on our own wagon trains to what for us really was the Promised Land, free of master, free of slavery, or so we prayed. We did not know so very much about the massacre of Native Americans or their harsh treatment under the lash in the hands of the priests, the reverends, cattle moguls, the best West Point had to offer, nor had we anticipated the Dred Scott decision.

The Dred Scott decision held ramifications that affected every black soul, free or slave, since the end result was that, according to Chief Justice Roger B. Taney, black people "had no rights which the white man was bound to respect." That meant a heyday for bounty hunters, fugitive slave hounds, and others who were determined to remand every African in sight to his master. And if there was no master to be found, "Get ye to the auction block" was a fine refrain. With all this hanging over their heads and many western states blatantly warning us that black labor was a blight that would not be tolerated in the still untamed territories. Those of us who did determine to head West were truly embarking on a quixotic journey, a very dangerous one. Even a poster encouraging movement westward stated in no uncertain terms: "Beware of speculators and Adventurers, as it is a dangerous thing to fall into their hands" (Nashville, Tennessee, March 1878).[1]

This was one reason Oklahoma became the focal point of so

many black folks' dreams. Oklahoma was not tainted with the legacy of John Brown's abolitionist radicals nor with roving bands of marauders, "bushwhackers," lost, without a cause following the War, except to keep Kansas "free of the dusky blight of niggers." The word *Oklahoma* took on the radiance of the "rapture" God-fearing black Christians sought fearlessly.

On July 22, 1891, A. G. Belton, a black southern entrepreneur, wrote to the American Colonization Society of his fervent sense that our post-slavery communities were still suffering from being what the Beatles might have called "Nowhere Men": "We as a people are oppressed and disenfranchised we are still working hard and our rights taken from us times are hard and getting harder every year. We as a people believe that Africa is the place but to get from under bondage we are thinking of Oklahoma as this is our nearest place of safety."[2]

Now we know some greater, more compassionate spirit, a Q-like figure, should have cautioned the mighty herds of bison, buffalo, and deer that ran freely over the lands west of the Mississippi. But that was not the case. Now, in order to get buffalo or venison, farm-raised or hunted only on specific days in specific numbers if at all, we must give our butchers a day or two notice. The black frontiersmen and their families, however, were traveling/settling in the land of plenty, if not the land of milk and honey. I am certain that just as we get excited about a beef pot roast for supper, a venison pot roast or buffalo stew was equally satisfying to our forebears.

We know that the first Africans traversed the country, the United States of America, with Spanish explorers. We also know that black soldiers, the Buffalo Soldiers, were definitively responsible for the containment and oppression of many Native American tribes. Where are their bones? How do we reconcile

going to Bonham, Texas, or Nicodemus, Kansas, without ac-
cepting that part of us which allowed for the further ravaging
of Indians, their lands and cultures? Some Africans can read
bones; even ground to powder, bones can reveal to some Africans in touch with the spirits what happened and what will
happen to those who disturb these bones of our people left so
long to an earned peace, an ironic freedom, impossible in this
world.

One spiritual recognizes the significance of them organic arti-
facts: "Dem bones, dem bones, dem dry bones"; yet another African culture, Cuba, was allowed to let the bones take on power.
Even though Elegua, the Yoruban Orisha of the Crossroads, is a
young and robust figure in Africa, in the New World Elegua is
transformed to an old, wizened character with a staff and the
frailty of Rwandan refugees. Thus we changed, made necessary
readjustments of our gods and belief systems to accommodate
the Christianity thrust upon us as our salvation. Someone apparently having overlooked the epistemological root of "salvation"
as "going home." In *Santería: African Spirits in America*, Joseph Murphy describes this metamorphosis.

> As they were leaving the palace [en La Habana] in order to leave
> room for the others they marched in perfect order. Congos and
> Lucumis with their great sombreros of feathers, vests with blue
> stripes and pants of red percale; Araras with their cheeks covered
> with scars cut with red-hot iron, bedecked with shells and the
> teeth of dogs and alligators, beads strung of bones and glass and
> their dancers had wrapped around their waists a big hoop cov-
> ered with raffia; Mandingas very elegant with their wide trou-
> sers, short jackets and turbans of blue or red silk, edged with mar-
> abu; and so many others, finally, with difficult names and fanciful
> clothes that were not adorned entirely in the African style, but re-
> formed or modified by civilized influence.[3]

Not long ago, along the nearly completed Vine Street Ex-
pressway in Philadelphia, workmen and anthropologists came
upon an entire collection of bones, bones of dead freedmen buried 'neath the rubble of a Chinatown in the midst of reconstruc-
tion or gentrification; again, point of view determines which. At
any rate, there was an absolute gasp of surprise and a wonder-
ment that enraged the Philadelphia community for days. Who
were these dead "colored" people? What were they doing underneath the Chinese people who were trying to build themselves a future? Why didn't we know they were down there?
Obviously, these free men and women of color missed or chose
not to hear the call to go West uttered by so many of their con-
temporaries or go back to Africa. Even the island of Cyprus; just
go 'way from here.

They didn't catch on, and so some many decades later people
with televisions, motorcars, and cyberspace chat rooms wondered what to do with them: the bones. Others wondered
whether it was moral to defile graves so long comforted by silence, stillness. I was one of them until I thought about the possibility that lots of Asian bones might, in fact, lie beneath ruins of
homesteads, ranches, the whole towns free people of color con-
structed for themselves west of the Mississippi, in hopes of sur-
viving their Manifest Destiny as blacks in America, while living
as free determining communities, when it wasn't yet apt to bring
property values down because we lived in densely small pockets
of the American frontier.

Bones of the dead are held sacred by most human communities; ours is no exception. But our bones had to be moved to make
room for "progress"; in the mid-to-late nineteenth century our
bones had to be moved, simply 'cause they were our bones which
were "degraded remains" of another lower species of man. This

happened anywhere the state or municipality declared eminent domain to achieve some greater goal, a railroad, a shopping center, a housing development. Our graves were regarded as little more than remnants of savages who'd contributed little if anything to the American Dream. I know this in a personal way, I think, for there are donations now being solicited to maintain the centuries of African-American cemetery where my forebears on my father's side have been and still are laid to rest. If living black folks can just be moved out of the way, what makes it so improbable that our dead would be treated any better? I still wonder how many Chinese laborers' bones lay beneath the route of the first transcontinental railroad, how many small black towns were built on them, what if any of them remain for us to salute/revere. What'd they eat? What'd they grow? Independent of a "master" to define the crop, its yield, its value, what part, if any, did we share?

freedom food

filadelfia
created some one
kinda freedom for some
one kinda folks what melanin
done left to burn in the sun and
have cancer and bury theyselves 3 deep
in DAR sanctified cemeteries / philadelphia left
us what got melanin to feed them / to save them from
yellow fever and the fire and the heat of
chimney flumes in winter / texas left
us slaves two years longer than
any darker folk / but
with freedom heah come land and

respect for survivin' what the
land demands of a people / I / yo acierta
plan to ride my words and pans to
freedom here in en tejas
where we pretty niggahs all bloom
like wildflowers
presente wit the gall a
appaloosas.

Does this in any way return to our experience before slavery, before the European, before what the world was to us was out of our control? See for yourself. Here, from an *odu*, a poem that suggests possible solutions to problems, according to Yoruba beliefs:

You are Oyeku
I am also Oyeku
Daylight is just appearing in the skies
But people thought it was already morning.
Ifa divination was performed for Fish
Who was the offspring of the riverbed.
Fish was told to perform sacrifice,
They told her that she would have many children,
But she was warned to perform sacrifice to prevent
attacks of human beings.
She did not perform sacrifice.
She said it was not possible for enemies
to see her children at the bottom of the river.[4]

Poor 'Liza in *Uncle Tom's Cabin* can attest otherwise. So can the mother of Emmett Till. But we are survivors and we must continue our journey.

CHAPTER 9

Better Late Than Never

*1910, Oklahoma enacted a grandfather clause that disen-
franchised its black citizens on the basis that their grand-
fathers, as slaves, had not voted. What law failed to accomplish in ending black independence, power and manhood
rights, whites achieved through fraud and violence ...
The black dream of Oklahoma became another southern
nightmare.*

WILLIAM LOREN KATZ,
The Black West

YET, WHAT COULD HAVE BEEN an even greater soul
trauma for black Texans ended as a magnificent celebration of *la liberté, l'égalité, la fraternité,* to borrow a phrase
from our Haitian brothers who were also hoodwinked outa real
freedom. It seems that the presence of Africans in Texas since the
sixteenth century, our intermingling with northern Mexicans for
no less than three centuries, and the illegal importation of thousands of native-born Africans from Cuba to Texas during the
mid-1800s failed as legitimate reasons to announce the "freeing
of the slaves," also known as the Emancipation Proclamation of
President Abraham Lincoln, September 22, 1862. While ignored throughout most of the Confederacy, enslaved Africans in

Texas were deliberately kept ignorant of their new status until June 19, 1867, when General Order number 3, authored by a Major General Granger, was issued without much ado.

GENERAL ORDER, NO. 3

> The people are informed that, in accordance with a proclamation from the Executive of the United States, all slaves are free. This involves an absolute equality of personal rights and rights of property, between former masters and slaves and the connection heretofore existing between them, becomes that between employer and hired labor. The Freedmen are advised to remain at their present homes and work for wages. They are informed that they will not be allowed to collect at military posts; and they will not be supported in idleness either there or elsewhere.[1]

Imagine the impact of such a sweeping change in a territory where, by 1860, Africans were clearly a third of the Texas population. And imagine they did. Since they'd missed the end of slavery by two years, black Texans created their own Independence Day, Juneteenth, which is still celebrated wherever black Texans and their descendants or admirers dwell, from oil-rich Alaska to the plains of Nebraska and Kansas. June 19 is a special day for us, a day of absence, we might say. A day of celebration.

Along with Mexican and mestizo cowpunchers, black cowboys and their women found ways of gettin' together and amusin' themselves that are still practiced today in far-off outa-the-way homesteads or urban cowboy enclaves from Las Vegas to Boise.

I haveta describe to ya a dazzlin' feat tol' to me by Dena Swayze, somebody who was actually there a couple of years ago in Colorado and whose attention to detail is truly astounding.

{60}

I was attending an outdoor trick roper and whip handler show, and the demonstration included volunteers. Let me tell ya, the handler pulled me out the crowd. There I was center stage, he's standin' there with two ten-foot whips to "tie" me up. He's six feet from me, understand? Cracked the first whip, and used that momentum after the crack to wrap up my ankles! Did the same thing with the second whip, but this time he got my wrists, since my arms were stretched out. Now, here, this must make me a fool. I'm standing there, all tied up already, when he puts a piece of spaghetti in my mouth and a blindfold over my eyes. What people tell me is, he snapped the spaghetti 'bout two inches from my lip. I was blindfolded, so I wouldn't flinch! Thank God.

The most spectacular arena was the rodeo where the wit, skill, and strength of real animals was challenged by black cowboys whose tradition in this arena was as old as their Mexican forebears. At least that's what I discovered when I added barrel racing, pole bending, roping, bulldoggers, tie-down, and bronco busters to my emotional and physical regimen. Along with modern dance classes in Sunnyside, a miniature Watts in Houston, came the challenge of learning to ride against a clock, partner a two-thousand-pound animal in a rough but precise tango with the wind, or a mean turn on four legs, my head and my horse's held proud, high, as expected of any Alvin Ailey dancer.

Rodeos provide the excitement and the time for women (usually, but not always) to prepare the finest barbecue of the season, while others demonstrate their prowess on horses with a mind of their own; the fires were stoked for traditional grilled meat from longhorn brisket to whole *cabritos* (young kids) spiked and rotating over a hot, smoldering fire.

Though just as the cry "There's gold in them thar hills" echoed across the continental United States, so did the hum

"There's oil in them thar hills," which changed how barbecues at rodeos were prepared. From empty oil piping, cut lengthwise, we developed a cooking machine where the heat could be controlled, the meat smoked and saturated in its own juices and wanton smoke not cloud the eyes of rodeo clowns seeking to protect a bulldogger trying to outdo Bill Pickett or a young barrel racer fighting the clock and the edges of upright oil drums. My good friend from Houston, Enomoyi Ama, describes one—or something like it.

> We saw one of Ben Stevenson's pits outside, chained outside, C. Anderson Davis's Bar. This was a five-foot straight piece welded together. The other kind is made of two two-foot sections and one three-foot section welded together, so you got two different levels. An interesting thing is that only pin hinges are used to attach the top to the bottom where the pit is covered with steel mesh; this is where the food lays. With these pin hinges, there are no loose little things sticking out. And if you want to take the top off, the whole thing comes off in one piece. Your firebox goes up under the steel mesh. Well, you know that.

Texas Shredded-Beef Barbecue

Cut 4–5 pounds meat in regular-size pieces. Mind to trim off extra fat and wash well. Soak this in cold water. The next mornin' hold your meat under cold running water (where possible) and dry. Take all this and your seasonings to the rodeo. Set up your grill so you're able to get a fairly high flame when you want. Heat ½ cup bacon fat and ½ stick butter (that's right) and sauté 1 large chopped onion. When the onion starts to brown add pieces of meat and seasoning and cook over low flames to start. Stir, adding a few drops of boiling water from time to time. When meat is brown and tender, almost dry, put in your salt and

1 large chopped bell pepper and set in a heavy mortar to be pounded till meat is shredded. (You can also do this by running your beef twice through a food grinder.) Then add your sauce.

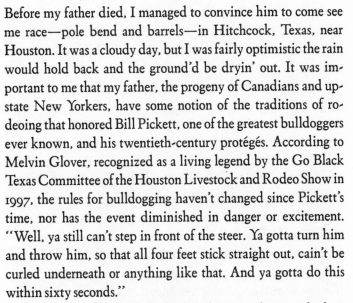

Before my father died, I managed to convince him to come see me race—pole bend and barrels—in Hitchcock, Texas, near Houston. It was a cloudy day, but I was fairly optimistic the rain would hold back and the ground'd be dryin' out. It was important to me that my father, the progeny of Canadians and up-state New Yorkers, have some notion of the traditions of rodeoing that honored Bill Pickett, one of the greatest bulldoggers ever known, and his twentieth-century protégés. According to Melvin Glover, recognized as a living legend by the Go Black Texas Committee of the Houston Livestock and Rodeo Show in 1997, the rules for bulldogging haven't changed since Pickett's time, nor has the event diminished in danger or excitement. "Well, ya still can't step in front of the steer. Ya gotta turn him and throw him, so that all four feet stick straight out, cain't be curled underneath or anything like that. And ya gotta do this within sixty seconds."

At any rate, the rain did hold, but the ground was soaked, so as to be dangerous for riders and animals alike. Nevertheless, there was plenty of barbecue to be had. Before we had to put a slab of plywood under the car to get her movin', Daddy did snidely remark, "Oh, I can make better barbecue sauce at home [New Jersey]." I came back with a quick jab. "Maybe so, but it won't be Texas beef." I didn't get to race barrels for my daddy that day, though I tried to explain the rules and skills to my very eastern father—the rules as I learned them from none other than

Melvin Glover, my walking cowpuncher encyclopedia. I went by the handle the Gypsy Cowgirl, which suited my poetic side, I thought. Anyway, Glover forever reminded me that (1) if I knocked over a barrel, that was an automatic five-second penalty; (2) if I broke my pattern, I was simply disqualified; (3) in some rodeos, if my horse or I came in contact with the barrels, there was some kinda penalty for that, too. So, insteada bein' able to concentrate on my prowess as a barrel racer and pole bender, Daddy got a dizzyin' delight, just thinkin' about his sauce.

Daddy's Barbecue Sauce

Add 1 can tomato paste to 2 cups orange juice with the pulp, ¼ cup Worcestershire sauce, and 3 tablespoons A-1 sauce. Then simmer over low flame. Get ⅓ cup Black Jack molasses or ½ cup brown sugar. Put that in there. Add salt and pepper to taste, 1 medium sautéed onion, 1 large hot pepper or 2 small sweet peppers. Let that sit for a while. Just before you add your meat or pour over your meat (in the case of ribs, shrimp, salmon, chicken, fluke, or bluefish), sling a dash of bourbon, red wine, or a golden tequila in there just for the hell of it. It's important that folks don't feel a need to add something to my sauce. Let the sauce cook with the meat (on it) until it becomes a part of the meat and doesn't slide off or peel off. That's when you can serve it.

I never revealed to my father that we can flavor the fire with mesquite or tequila as well as other herbs, which work just as well to season the meats and vegetables with a magical taste; makes you think that's how they come naturally. Plus, my father missed the discovery that meat from longhorn cattle, ostrich, and buffalo is lower in fat, more tender, and just as good as something you didn't hunt yourself.

What's amazing to me, though I guess it shouldn't be, is that our compatriots in Trinidad and Tobago used these same oil barrels that we use to barbecue to make steel drums, ranging in tonality from tympani to well above high C, from which emanate Beethoven or the Mighty Sparrow, the calypsonian.

> To make your steel pan you need a 45-gallon oil drum, a sledgehammer, a small hammer, metal punch, ruler, compasses, and chalk. The unopened end of the oil drum is "sunk" with the sledgehammer, deeper for the higher drums and shallower for the cello and bass pans. The position of the notes (around the perimeter and in center) is outlined with compasses and chalk and then beaten out with a hammer and tempered with fire and water. The final tuning is carefully done with a small hammer and a rubber-tipped playing stick.[2]

So, as David Rudder says, "It's a pan man's war," or in my case a barbecue war, followed by hours of dancing, either the Trinidad and Tobago Jump-Up or the Texas Two Step. Though no rodeo is real rodeo, calves, no calves, food, no food, without the legendary line dance the Cotton-eyed Joe, which does resonate with the ring shout, swing, and square dance. Our people rode with Billy the Kid from the Northern Plains down past the Mexican border. Rufus Buck's gang rivaled the Daltons in misdeeds and daring; further south in the Caribbean, we produced C. L. R. James and Eric Williams, intellectual renegades. So what we eat fueled all that. That's a cue to me 'bout what to keep in my kitchen, 'round my oil-pipe barbecue as I wiggle to the pan man and make my good sense fall down to the under the ground.

I didn't know all of this when I first started going to Texas in the mid-seventies to work at the Equinox Theatre; I was in a state of awe. Even more so than when I'd driven across country, stopped in Amarillo, found a café with a real cinema, real red-and-white-checked tablecloths, and a waitress who looked like Karen Black with a South Philadelphia Italian girl's version of Brigitte Bardot's classic hairdo. I immediately turned to walk out, but the waitress entreated me, in a sweet voice only southern women have mastered, to please stay for lunch. I did, while looking vigilantly for Klansmen or the bikers who shot Peter Fonda. I musta misunderstood the very kind Texas woman because I was totally unprepared for chicken-fried steak. All I knew about was chicken fried like chicken or fish fried like fish, but not one animal fried like another kind of animal. At any rate, I didn't send this "new" dish back to the kitchen, where a husky black guy was obviously waiting to see how much care he'd invested in my meal. No indeed.

I was raised to experiment with taste and sound, thus my interest in music, language, and food, but more importantly to never turn my nose or chin up to any kinda food that anybody ate. First of all, who was I to do such a thing. Secondly, they must like whatever they're enjoying eating. So it was a matter of respect. I had my first chicken-fried steak in Amarillo in June of 1974, thinking I was experiencing what Blanche Boyd might call a white-trash classic. To my surprise, the longer I stayed around and about the Southwest, with my relatives or on my own, chicken-fried steak is one of those things everybody does, like New Yorkers of any nationality can tell a Hebrew National hot dog from Oscar Mayer. It's a simple concept. However, there is a "colored" way to make yourself a chicken-fried steak. I am now goin'ta share my way with you.

I believe in using choice pieces of meat, though that's not always possible or necessary. Anyway, with a decent piece of sirloin steak that's been tenderized by piercing with a fork or pounding, cut vertical slits in the rim of fat along the edge so your meat won't curl up. If you want to be really fancy, this meat can be marinated in Worcestershire sauce, red wine, or a mesquite-tinged hot sauce. Meanwhile, fix a batter of milk, eggs, flour (you can add crushed pecans or walnuts to the same batter we use to fry okra—see page 75), salt, and pepper. Dredge your meat on both sides in the batter in a thick-bottom frying pan, the old-fashioned kind, I guess. Your oil should be hot so that a sprinkle of water sizzles. The same problem that confronts you when you are frying chicken appears here. We don't want the crust of the meat to brown too quickly, before the meat is done. That requires you to mediate the range of the fire 'neath your pan with some focus. I like my meat rare, so my steak is in and out as soon as the crust is a fine brown. I don't know what to tell you if you want your meat well done. I imagine you'll be at the stove a bit longer.

Chicken-fried Steak

I'm including chicken-fried steak that goes wonderfully with grits and cheese or for late supper with creamed spinach and mashed potatoes and cheese because African-American settlers who might have followed men like "Pap" Singleton to Kansas or gone to Oklahoma and West Texas were hunters, and serious beef eaters, like most ranchers are. Therefore, a fine meal is a fine meal, whether the homesteader is black or white. It'll just taste different 'cause we're different.

CHAPTER 10

Is That Why the Duke
Had a Train of His Own?

H OW TO EAT TO LIVE" was one of the Honorable
Elijah Muhammad's most popular columns in *Muhammad Speaks* (*Bilalian News*), yet what if at some
point during our sojourns in the New World we decided we did
not want to eat to live: that we did not want to live at all?

There is a scene in the immensely successful *Foxes of Harrow*,
by the often neglected black writer Frank Yerby, in which a
young woman flees from the auction area, running to the sea,
where death/freedom await. The master, played by an ex-
tremely young Rex Harrison, encourages his favorite manservant
(read slave) to go after her. The willfulness displayed, preferring
to face a ruthless ocean rather than a ruthless slavery, was looked
upon with perverse favor. This, at a time when Stepin Fetchit
and housemaids with the brains of peas looked after the likes of
Jean Harlow and Katharine Hepburn, was an attempt to see slavery as we saw it and to see ourselves outside and inside the imbe-
cilic stereotypes Hollywood studios deemed adequate for "our
kind."

Yerby's defiant and self-determining characters, though enslaved, engaged in passionate and idealistic romance. The young
man chased the wench 'cross hill and dale till he'd made her
"his," at which point she had to eat, as she was with child. This

union in the distorted world of plantation life left their offspring, L'il Inch, lame in one leg, but nevertheless honored from his toddler years to look after and play with the precious child of the master and mistress of the big house. Yerby's refusal to live in the United States, his fair complexion, and his bold attempts to examine antebellum Southern life did not gain him much popularity among the black bourgeoisie who were hell-bent on forgetting everything and anything associated with slavery, which meant forgetting themselves, forgetting to feed the ancestors, or us.

Refusing to eat, however, was one of the many methods Africans used to maintain some dignity, some control of their lives. This was so to the extent that both British and Portuguese slavers had words and explanations for an African's refusal to accept nourishment. Kenneth F. Kiple and Brian T. Higgins write in their essay "Mortality Caused by Dehydration during the Middle Passage" in *The Atlantic Slave Trade*:

> The English lumped a strange array of maladies together; heat sickness, dysentery, apathy, weakness, muscle cramps, emaciation, sunken eyes, and delirium, and called it "fixed melancholy." The Portuguese termed it *banzo* and both thought it quite deadly ... A Brazilian dictionary defined banzo as "the mortal melancholy that attacks the blacks from Africa," mortal because slaves seemed to retreat into themselves and successfully will themselves to die. .... Africans, unlike other peoples, could commit suicide by holding their breath. Modern writers, on the other hand, have tended to view the condition as a "state of shock" which led to an "involuntary suicide" and one has wondered if medical science has ever known of such a phenomenon.[1]

If we wander our streets at random, we can ourselves wonder at the recurrence of banzo in the persons of those crackheads, dope fiends, and homeless bewildered among us. Sunken eyes and emaciation make the grade for me. So banzo is in full-blown epidemic swing, though few among us could name it. It is the will to die.

I'm sure crackheads and dope fiends don't consider themselves to be among the smoke and mirrors that surrounded any discussion of slavery, but they are. In the same way that Raul Zurita's beautiful poems escape from airplane fuels into the air and disappear. What we want of our world and what we have offered stand in clear opposition. We want nothin'. On the other hand, we continually make somethin' outa nothin.'

If life offers no possibilities that we can discern, we cook heroin, crack, crank, something just for ourselves, that get us away from everybody, lets us be alone, malnourished and quietly dying over our fires. Cooking is a way of insisting on living, much in the same way that banzo was a way to refuse a life without the flavor of freedom. When we are hungry for life, we search out spices, aromas, and texture to entice and please those around us.

Take for instance gumbo. The two most significant popularizers of gumbo are Charleston and New Orleans. For two obvious reasons: (1) the presence of the French before the British; (2) the presence of large numbers of first-generation Africans fresh off the boat, so to speak. Who would not delight in a dish of fresh gumbo after a rationed diet of boiled horse beans, rice, corn, yams, or even manioc, in some combination laced with red peppers? Now, Carolinian gumbos generally have a reddish hue to them, while Louisiana gumbos range from café au lait to deep browns. We're apt to find more vegetables in Carolinian gumbos than the other, as well. This must be a regional peculiarity, because they certainly have vegetables in Louisiana. Nevertheless, there are two ingredients to a gumbo that must be present or we've got a soup on our hands and no gumbo at all: okra and roux. In his essay "French Creoles on the Gulf Coast," in *To Build a New Land: Ethnic Landscapes in North America*, Phillipe Oszuscik tells us of gumbo:

> Many variations exist, including seafood, poultry, and vegetarian. In all of them, one begins with a roux, a base for gravies and sauces and a thickener of French origin. It is made of butter (or oil) and flour. A soup must have either seafood or okra, a vegetable that originated in Africa, or both, to qualify as a true gumbo. The word "gumbo" may have been derived from the African word "guingombo," meaning "okra," or from the Choctaw word "kombo," meaning "file" (ground sassafras leaves). Okra was the African contribution, cayenne peppers were added to the recipe by the Spanish, and file was contributed by the Gulf Coast Indians.[2]

Now a roux is not just some butter and flour or oil and flour. A roux is the embodiment of the soul of a family. There's much more there than can be recounted to someone unfortunate enough to not be "blood." Grandmothers threaten to fly in circles over the bed, mothers swear they'll turn your weddin' dress red, or even, God forbid, black, if the secrets of a family roux are ever, and I do mean *ever*, revealed.

Miss Marie, my inveterate friend from South Texas, told me to go on ahead and make me a roux till it taste right to me. That was so helpful. Anyway, I do know that after mixing the flour with the butter (oil), at some point garlic, onion, bell pepper, and corn may be added. This does not mean that other ingredients like celery, hot peppers, shallots, or pimiento aren't added. Until the taste of one's roux overwhelms your senses, makes you silly with gluttony, I guess the roux isn't quite right. It's important to remember to throw out, yes, throw out, a roux that's been burnt too dark. Just get rid of it and start over. Eventually, a roux simmering at a particular texture, a particular color will suit your fancy. You can declare that your family secret. I know one old woman who makes her roux in the middle of the night and buries it outside where no one can find it. That way a soul with an acute sense of smell can't make out what's in the roux.

It's easier to get your okra ready for your gumbo. The most important thing is not to put your okra in the gumbo too soon. If the okra cooks as long as everything else, then, yes, the okra'll be gooey and stringy, virtually disappearing in the sauce, which crab, lobster, shrimp, and clam don't do. Even if the meat falls off the chicken bone, there's more to it than a healthy okra fallin' away from itself. Before you start cookin', make sure your okra is fresh, green (no brown or black blemishes). You can chop your okra or slice it or leave it whole in its natural beauty. This recipe was prepared for me by my uncle Eric F. Lum, Sr., of Charleston, South Carolina, and Queens, New York.

1 WHOLE chicken, diced, not necessarily deboned
1 LB sausage
1 CUP fresh green peas
1 CUP sweet corn
1 LB okra
4–6 tomatoes
½ DOZEN crabs
1 LB shrimp, lobster, scallops, oysters, clams, if you like

*Uncle Eric's
Gumbo
(Carolinian)*

First, you make your roux (I can't share mine with you now), but you got your roux cookin'. In some other pots, brown your chicken parts, your sausage, or boudin [blood sausage], which-ever. Take your peas, corn, your okra to be sure, and hold them by the wayside. Chop you some pretty tomatoes. Add all this to your roux with some water and a dash of whiskey. Put your vege-tables and seafoods in last so they don't overcook. Crabs, shrimps, and such can go right in with their shells. Otherwise you'll be up forever taking those shells apart. Let the folks eating your gumbo enjoy themselves, pulling the meat out of those things. You must got enough sense to make you a pot of rice. Pour your gumbo over your rice. That's all I can tell you.

I was stunned when I had my first bowl of Louisiana gumbo, that it was brown and that there wasn't a bed of rice cradling the meats and okra, the way my family's did. I felt my heart falling. I knew my hosts were offering me their gumbo, but it wasn't gumbo. Aside from the makin' of boudin, I've seldom encoun-tered a food that drives the primordial southern soul more than gumbo. Maybe because so many of us have such a stake in it. It's a food that couldn't exist without us.

This is why the restitution of okra's reputation is one of my projects. I love okra and my soul is shaken every time I see some-one turn her head in disgust, hang his head down like someone's done somethin' to be ashamed of because we're havin' okra for supper. I do not understand this. I refuse to allow our own people to reject an Africanism that is not inanimate or residual. Okra is one of our living ties to the motherland. In celebration I might make me a parade or an Okra Day/Are You Black or Not?

Wash 1 pound of okra real well, like all other vegetables, in cold water. Then chop the top thick ends off. Discard. The rest of the okra is fine for cookin'. Chop your lovely fresh okra into slices 'bout an inch wide, including the cute little ends. They'll fry just fine. Now, you can make you a batter of ½ cup of cornmeal, ⅔ cup milk, and 1 egg to dip the okra in before fryin'. Or you can simply dip the okra in some milk, run it through flour or cornmeal fast as lightning, then fry. Butter is great, but you'll need a lot of it to get the okra the right color brown. So try some regular household oil like Crisco or Mazola. Before you put your okra in to fry, make sure water sizzles in the grease. Make sure that you've got a good, heavy fryin' pan, so the okra doesn't stick to the bottom and burn on one side, gettin' stuck to the metal. Let your fried okra drain in some paper towels, so it's not greasy to the taste. There, we've got a batch of fine fried okra. With seasoning to taste, you can eat it like popcorn or let it take its place as a dinner vegetable.

Fried Okra

Yes, this is one of my favorites. When I smell this cookin' (even if I'm cookin' it myself), tears well up in my eyes. Now, I'm not goin' to condescend to you every time we attempt some recipe by reminding you to wash the food and your hands; this time, however, I will make a blanket statement. Always wash the food before you cook it. Always wash your hands. Continually, so that the smell of one food doesn't contaminate another. Rinse your utensils for the same reason.

Okra, Tomatoes, Corn, and Onions

1 LB okra
3–4 CLOVES garlic
1–2 deseeded peppers
3 small onions
3 EARS corn
5–6 small tomatoes

This is not a complicated recipe at all. Chop your garlic, peppers (habañero or jalapeño or pobalano), and onions. Sauté this in a pan of butter. Rake the corn off the cobs. Yes, that's right. Do not buy yourself a can of sweet corn. Take the sweet corn off the cob yourself. Much better that way. Then you can slice your okra into one-inch segments or leave the okra in its natural state. Chop up your tomatoes; I prefer plum tomatoes. When your onion and garlic are nearing a clear coloring, drop your okra in the pan. Don't add your corn or tomatoes till the okra is just about tender as you desire. Corn and tomatoes have a tendency to disappear with too much cookin'. Now, your peppers should always maintain their shape (thus, their taste). It's optional, whether to throw in a dash of white wine toward the end of the preparation. Can't hurt, though. This can be served alone or over rice or vermicelli.

There's no reason why okra can't be used raw in salads, or broiled with peppers and onions on a grill in summer. It's virtually treason not to enjoy (exploit) the little bit of Africa that's actually cultivated in this country.

Okra fills out just about any kind of stew or fricassee just right. Any sautéed or broiled seafood sits right with it as well, especially oysters and clams.

This will come as no surprise to my sister, who spent time in Guinea and knows whereof I speak. On the other hand, alas, my immediate family has left the poor African okra to other palates, grand receipts, and holiday tables to fend for itself. Too sticky, stringy, slimy, bitter, and so on, the complaints go. None of these petty observations apply if you've cooked your okra in the manners suggested. I know this. I eat okra. I eat okra a lot. I think we should free the okra, the way we freed the watermelon. And Duke Ellington freed bass and treble clefs, feet and torsos, and any constricting images of royalty.

CHAPTER II

And What Did You Serve?
Oh, No, You Did Not!

EVER SINCE my first encounters with boys (read young men), my great-aunt's and my grandmother's first queries were not what did we do (though they should have been), nor what did we talk about but what did I serve the boy. Sometimes, I said soda pop or lemonade and chips, or sometimes I said, "Nothing." It was bad enough that I had to come inside to "entertain" instead of wandering 'round the neighborhood, taking adventurous rides alongside the trolley tracks, through alleys, down rich people's rolling lawns, finding a field where we imagined ourselves the first human beings, I had to feed him, too?

Eventually, I realized that my elders had in mind something more akin to ancient mating rituals than what we call dating. As if I should offer at least sweet potato pie with ice cream, not store-bought cookies and Kool-aid. This to prove I was of value, valued my visitors and our time together so much that I made a hands-on effort to create something for whoever this person was. After fifteen, these offerings were not to be insubstantial, either, "Well, didn't you offer him some turkey, or a bowl of chowder, some greens and ham hocks?" I began to feel a bit incompetent. The solution, stop having company.

Now I understand that I was being initiated into a very southern/African tradition of sharing the best I had with visitors, to show our generosity, good faith, and appreciation of their experiences as individuals, for all this breaking of bread was enmeshed with the exchange of travelers' stories, family mythology, *bochinche* (gossip), and speculations on the political and economic future of the Negro. I don't know why I didn't catch on sooner.

As my Aunt Effie used to say, "Oh, you've got to have food in the house, child. You never know who's comin'." In these days and times, that could be a fairly threatening statement, but what she meant I now understand and feel compelled to act out, although I do know that most of the time nobody is coming. Yet, when my house starts to smell like no one's cookin' in it, no one's sighed deeply after a dish of blueberry cobbler or sweet potato puffs, I find myself questioning my own value, what I value, what is a well-lived life. I miss the ritual of a good meal that is shared. In our family, first there were the stories, bringing everyone up to date on the most courageous/outrageous of our blood, our clan, so to speak. This is a very African process, falling in line with the works of griots/praise-song singers. Even if a minute piece of information had been discovered about Lizzie, Maria, or Sister, that detail had to be put in context with the entirety of the passel of legend that is us. So that snippet of gossip, discovery of an outside child, a pair of red patent stilettos, a sudden disappearance, readjusts the whole of our mythology, reshapes our tale. As we approach the millennium, the Owens and Williams clans, together or alone, make testimony similar to this ancestral call of the Twi.

Odomankoma
Created the thing
The generous hewer-out

He created the herald
He created the drummer
He created "touch and die"
The executioner
And they all claim
To have come from one pod
Come, herald, and receive
Your Colobus-monkey skin cap!
And what was your heritage?[1]

And we soak up these words, new images of ourselves from the visitor, the travelers who shall be fed and entertained by us with gratitude. Yes, as modern as we imagine ourselves to be with our modems and microwaves, there's nothing quite like an eighty-year-old third cousin swearing I favored Mary Etta as a child, when I'm busy nearing middle age and would I please chop that celery over there. Magic has always been associated with the mixing of things, some congruent, others baffling. I find these elements in midnight/dawn family gatherings when maybe rum, Johnny Walker Black instead of *aguardiente* (sugar-cane liquor), so cherished throughout Latin America, in small quantities, of course, just like palm wine in the motherland is, are slowly sipped as our story moves from one expert to the next. To be an expert we simply have to know something of the tellers of the tale, the rhythm of mixing the ingredients that nourish us. "Who told you you could use the tops of those green onions in my stew? Nobody I ever knew! Don't know where you got that from. Lord knows, I can't understand some of your ways."

But we mustn't forget the music, the latest hormonal-driven gyrations of the youngsters among us whose job it is to take our minds off their chopping, stirring, kneading, and waiting that a good meal demands. And while I've never feasted with the Twi, I've been blessed to have broken bread with Wolof, Zulu, and Yoruba. Although adjusted for "the ones who were lost" (descendants of the Diaspora, that's us), the dynamics of the reunion were terribly familiar. Even my three-year-old was swooped up in the depth of our joy in Dakar, spontaneously joining the male warriors as they danced, aggressively letting us know we were safe with them. She did the same with cousins in Texas who were deliberately showing off their new sexual powers doing the butterfly. And so, for now, we are not virtual families, but sense memories of movement, aroma, accents, and tastes peculiar to the hands of our blood relations. I emphasize bloodlines because, unlike dogs or horses, pedigree slaves were few and far between.

Anyway, an amazing energy breaks out between the kitchen and the dining room in the midst of simmering stews, roasts, or fried anything. You know, you can fry just about anything. Even fried corn bread/hush puppies.

Fried Corn *We need somewhere about 1 cup yellow cornmeal (which is*
Bread / Hush *thicker, grainier in texture than* harina de maize *or white corn-*
Puppies *meal or cornstarch), ⅓ cup sugar (white or light brown), just a*
tad of water. Mix these all up, then add 2 sprigs chopped pars-
ley, 4 finely diced green onions/scallions, ⅓ cup buttermilk,
and 2½ cups water—add gradually. Then simmer over me-
dium heat. All this will get heavy, but not lumpy if you minded
to stir it every so often. Turn the heat off. Ladle the dough into a
shallow pan. Let it cool. While it's cooling, heat up hot oil/fat 2

inches deep in pan. Pick a spoon, large or small, depending on how we want our hush puppies to look. Gently drop these spoonfuls into the hot oil until the ball is golden brown. Take it out of the oil. Set it to drain or eat immediately with or without butter.

Now, I can't say how many things you can eat hush puppies with, but this stew from the Caribbeans who married into or out of our family has certainly found a home with us.

According to the story as told by my fourth cousin's wife, Maribel, this stew is centuries old and was a staple among criollos, regardless of the changes in colonial rulers. We need a lot of things, so expect to spend one-half day just shopping, one-third resting, and a couple of hours actually cooking. Right away we have to desalt 2 pounds of tasajo *(salt-cured beef). When that's done, add 1 large flank steak, chopped, along with 3 pounds of deboned short ribs cut to 1-inch slices, with a bay leaf and bring to boil in a large pot, again removing any of the gray bubbling fat that comes to the top. In another pan make your sofrito. Everybody has one or more of these mixtures that's not unlike a roux, when you think about it. I'm going to tell you one that works for me. Heat 4 tablespoons olive oil until you can smell it steaming. Bring the heat down and sauté 1 large chopped red onion, 6 cloves garlic, and 1 large bell pepper. Mess it around in the pan so that nothing sticks to the bottom, just under 10 minutes. Then you can add 4–5 tomatoes (whole, chopped, canned, or fresh), 1 teaspoon cumin, and cook another few minutes. Over a mild*

You Know
What That
New Wife
Makes for
Brother's
Stew (Ajiaco)

{83}

heat add the sofrito to the meats, stirring all the while. Now we can add your vegetables at every few minutes in the following order:

> 1 *malanga amarillo* (yellow taro), peeled and quartered
> 1 peeled yucca in 2-inch slices
> 1 big green plantain, peeled and sliced
> 1 large white sweet potato (*boniato*), peeled and cut into 2-inch chunks (Do not use the sweet potato we're used to. It will fall to pieces in the cooking.)
> 1 big white malanga, peeled and quartered
> 1 tropical yam near the size of a medium white potato (Again, leave our yams and sweet potatoes out of this.)
> 1 really ripe plantain, peeled and sliced
> 1 CUP full of peeled and seeded *calabaza* or butternut squash
> 2 large ears corn, without husks and sliced

Now, you can sit down and let the whole thing simmer for about an hour. Then and only then can you add the corn. Serve hot and enjoy with your hot hush puppies. Serves 6–8.

We have to remember that we are a strangely worldly people, in spite of our so-called life in the ghetto, a quarter of a city in which Jews were required to live. We come from all over and take in strangers fluidly. Our men and women have served in every war the United States has waged: the Revolutionary War, the War of 1812, the Civil War, the Spanish-American War, World War I, World War II, the Korean War, the Vietnam War, the Gulf War, invasions of Nicaragua, Panama, the Dominican Republic, Haiti, Grenada, Bosnia, Somalia, and on and on. Sometimes we bring home people who've come to be known as war brides or war husbands (think Cary Grant).

When they mingle bloodlines with us, their children are part of us, their foods our foods. As Calypsonian Supreme, "The Watchman," sings in "My People":

When you're black you're black you're black
You'll always have a knife placed firmly 'gainst your back.

Nowhere was this more the truth than South Africa during apartheid, where the commingling of races and cultures was illegal and actual. From KwaZululand after Nelson Mandela's rise to the presidency, I traveled through South Africa, looking, dancing, writing, and eating. My favorite cities, Durban and Capetown, offered panoplies of the possibilities of the species given freedom to love and work without looking over our backs, suspicious of difference, the "other." No matter how philosophical we become here, South Africa is a land with a future others might envy. What is home here is known, maybe not immediately within our grasp, but known. In this arena food is a true connection to the past and what is to be as well as all that went between. South Africans are big meat eaters, but I've chosen a fish dish I adore for your palates.

Use enough olive oil or peanut oil to cover bottom of frying pan Fish Curry
by ½ inch to fry 1 medium onion. Then add 4 crushed garlic cloves, 1–2 chopped deseeded chili peppers, a bit of red masala *and green* masala *(hot spices to heat the body) available at any*

East Indian specialty store. Dashes of cardamom, cinnamon, cumin, pepper, nutmeg, 1 tablespoon curry powder, ½ tablespoon turmeric, 1 cup tomato sauce, thick, ½ cup puréed tomatoes, and 2 tablespoons sugar. Cook mixture until blended. Then gently add 2 pounds firm white fish in chunks, along with 1 cup coconut milk (canned or the real thing), and a little salt. Cook until fish flakes away from fork. At finish, garnish with fresh coriander. Serve with rice. And don't you fret. There are so many stories to tell.

CHAPTER 12

Virtual Realities,
Real People, Real Foods

No, it is no more soil than it is race which makes a nation. The soil furnishes the substratum, the field of struggle and labour, man furnishes the soul. Man is everything in the formation of this sacred thing which is called people . . . A nation is a soul, a spiritual principle.

HOMI BHABHA,
Nation and Narration

ALTHOUGH W. E. B. DU BOIS wrote *The Souls of Black Folk* and Margaret Walker blessed us with the classic *For My People,* we remain a concept of sorts without the substratum of soil. What our fate or visions would be, had the mythological "forty acres and a mule" been a reality, is "such stuff as dreams are made on." In the meantime, we've had to circumvent the realities of place and language to re-create a "where" for our people. I am referring here to the tens of thousands of African-Americans who are committed to an "other" way of life besides the American way. Rather than being imprisoned as the perceived other, we have embraced this as an opportunity that turns inward on itself and grows with the density and

{87}

influences of a black hole in space. Black nationalists, black Jews, and black Muslims have had a profound effect on the daily lives of all classes of mainland African-Americans, as well as those of us spread throughout the hemisphere.

I'll never forget the young man on a cliff outside Cancún, Mexico, who wove me a bamboo flute because I had a headful of African braids and this *flaco* (young man), handsome as he wanted to be, a headful of dreadlocks. He was a Rastafarian so far from Jamaica, I wondered did he pledge his submission to Jah, the deified figure of Haile Selassie, Lion of Judah, Ruler of Ethiopia, until his death not so many years ago. I wondered was he, too, one of us stranded in the New World to whom the Lion of Judah, Haile Selassie I, had promised our forty acres and a mule, if only we made it to the Promised Land. Generally, Rastafarians are vegetarian and whether in Cartagena or Kingston come together for the rituals of community that we call culture: music, song, dance, and food. Although as scholar Wole Soyinka noted in his critique of Ali Mazrui, "A quite unsubtle slant of denigration of the African past was effectively introduced, leaving the African values with no narrated strength its validity to contest or rationally accommodate the invading beliefs or retain any substance, depth, or relevance to African contemporary needs."[1]

Yet, definitively unstable measures were taken to ensure the further destabilization of African cultures during the time of slavery, which lasted in the New World until 1888 (Brazil). Religious ceremonies, rites of passage, food proscriptions, were trampled by slave owners in their futile attempts to dehumanize a people. Suspicions of our desire for freedom led to violent, sometimes insidious suppression of our expressions of ourselves. Not only were the Rastafarians in Jamaica regarded as dangerous, they were harassed and publicly humiliated as a rule. This is nothing new. In Brazil in 1835, something known as the Revolt of the Males was

an urban rebellion that broke out in Salvador . . . led by Muslim Nago slaves, more than seventy African slaves and freemen died during the uprising . . . The Revolt of the Males was the largest urban slave revolt in the history of the Americas, and left an en-during legacy of fear . . . As in the Western world of the late twentieth century, a deep distrust of Arabic language and Is-lamic religion pervaded Bahia.[2]

What better way to humiliate and break the spirits of such saboteurs than to limit their diet to pork, a food forbidden to Muslims and restricted to specific occasions by many African religions.

A dear friend of mine, Yvette Smalls, a Master Braider and videographer, generously shared her thoughts and recipes with us, as one hundred and some odd years later she and her family attempt to dignify the suffering and struggle of our forebears in bondage whenever they break bread.

Wheatmeat, the ingredient in wheat flour that allows dough to rise, can be easily obtained at any health food store. It looks like a good piece of steak without the veins.

Company's Comin' Wheatmeat with Organic Brown Rice / Good Salad

2 LB wheatmeat
3–4 TBS Bragg's Liquid Amino Acids
1–2 TSP garlic powder
1–2 TSP onion powder
1–2 TSP dulse (optional)
PINCH cayenne or curry for spicy flavor

Cut or slice wheatmeat into desired style. Pour sesame or safflower or any cold pressed oil into pan. Sauté 3–4 raw garlic cloves until brown. Remove from the pan. Now put wheatmeat into the pan. Allow it to brown 2–3 minutes. Then stir it around. Next, add your seasoning of garlic powder, onion powder, Bragg's, dulse, curry or cayenne.

Organic Brown Rice

4 cups spring or distilled water to 2 cups brown rice. Rinse rice in cold water. Then drain. Pour rice into pot and cover. Stir rice with fork once when it begins to boil. After it begins to boil turn flame down low. Allow 45–60 minutes for rice to cook or allow water to cut out of (evaporate from) pot and turn off. Stir all the seasonings in the wheatmeat. Allow to cook for approximately 7–10 minutes, depending on desired texture, soft or crunchy. Turn off heat and cover until rice is ready.

Good Salad

1–2 HEADS romaine lettuce
1 BUNCH spinach
2–4 STALKS celery
4–6 large carrots
1 red pepper or 1 HEAD broccoli
1 CONTAINER sprouts (any kind)

Wash all vegetables thoroughly. Cut or tear off bottom of lettuce. Tear leaves into small pieces. Put into large or medium-size bowl. Next rinse spinach. Cut off bottom tips. Tear leaves, then put in bowl. Cut off bottoms of celery. Cut lengthwise, then chop

*in small pieces. Add to bowl. Grate carrots with grater. Cut the
red pepper lengthwise. Chop off the bottoms of the broccoli. Toss
the salad. Garnish with sprouts.*

I confess that after my experiments with *Macrobiotics, You Are
What You Eat,* and various "Negroized" Hindu recipes, I gave
up vegetarianism the day I found I was so peaceful and passive I
let six A trains pass by me in Manhattan because too much aggressive energy was required for me to get myself through the
crowds. But I asked Yvette, "Why? We've got McDonald's,
Popeye's, Stouffer's, et cetera. Why go to all this trouble?" She
answered,

> I have chosen this lifestyle as an alternative to the diet suggested
> by America, which consists mostly of meat and dairy products.
> It is very nutritious, doesn't clog the colon or arteries, and, it is
> important to note, easily digested by the body!
>   I choose not to support the American death ceremony. Dis-
> ease begins in the body, but it is largely due to toxic chemicals, et
> cetera, in the food. I choose to eat live, healing foods that will en-
> sure longevity as well as spiritual balance, mental alertness, and
> physical strength.

One could also say that racism is toxic, so by metaphorically refusing an all-American diet of meat and potatoes, Yvette and
thousands of others refuse to swallow what will, in fact, poison
them: self-hatred. Maybe this is twentieth-century enlightened
bonzo. We are daring to live, to eat to live in honor of those who
decided to waste away as opposed to becoming who we are.
    Are we, as Molefi Asante ironically teases, made-in-America
Negroes, or are we, as the principle of Njia suggests, a people in

transition? In Euro-America there are two obvious examples of movements of people who, coming together with common beliefs and rituals, have survived *The Price Is Right* and cellular phones, the Mormons and the Amish. Among Afrocentrists an analogous dynamic is present. For instance, in this ceremony that usually takes place on Sundays, thus not disrupting daily life for ordinary people, Molefi Asante cites an invocation to the ancestors that designates us as carriers of a legacy that does not belong to us, but is of us.

> LIBATOR: We call upon our ancestors far and near, father of our fathers
> AUDIENCE: Mother of our mothers
> LIBATOR: To render mercy
> AUDIENCE: To bear witness
> LIBATOR: To the liberation and victory of our people
> AUDIENCE: Forever
> LIBATOR: It is done! (The libator pours water from the red vase into the black vase which should be in the middle position)[3]

On the other hand, we may be Africans in the Americas whose ties to our past were never broken or shredded, but merely dismissed as so much evidence of our barbarity and who owned us, even on their own feast days, the Cuban Twelfth Day.

> Each tribe, having elected its "king" and "queen," paraded the streets with a flag . . . The whole gang was under the command of the negro marshal, who, with a drawn sword, having a small piece of sugar-cane stuck on its point, was continually on the move to preserve the order in the rank. But the chief object in the groups was an athletic negro, with a fantastic straw helmet, an immensely thick girdle of strips of palm leaves around his waist

and other uncouth articles of dress. Whenever they stopped, their banjoes struck up one of their monotonous tunes, and this frightful figure would commence a devil's dance which was the signal for all his court to join in a general fandango, a description of which my pen refuseth to give.[4]

No wonder so many of us tried and some succeeded in running off to isolated communities, *quilimbos* in Brazil, "maroon" en-claves in Jamaica, Florida, Suriname, Colombia, Venezuela, where, not having accepted our very lives as spectator sports, we could go about our business. We are still able to accomplish this ability to live with some dignity in the privacy of our own homes when and where the Fourth Amendment to the Constitution is respected. Here, we may continue to erect family shrines, feed the spirits of our ancestors, root our children in traditions centu-ries old and unsullied. Our parents and theirs before them must be fed, just as the deities must feast on their birthdays, as we do: no particular delineation made between the world we inhabit or the world of the spirits; we're all here. While this is quite appar-ent in the African novels *The Palm Wine Drinkard* by Amos Tutola and Nigerian Ben Okri's *The Famished Road*, we must sometimes look about the homes of friends for the presence of those from "the other side," or *las siete potencias* (the seven powers) generically known as the orishas. Elegua, Ogun, Shango, Obatala, Yemeya, Oshun, and Oya, the Santerian pan-theon of gods who guide, protect, and determine our fates under the watchful gaze of Orunmilla, God Almighty.

Each orisha appears in glory on the feast day of his or her Catho-lic counterpart: Shango on Barbara's 4 December; Oshun on the Virgin's 8 September; Babaluye on Lazarus' 17 December. An-niversaries of initiation are celebrated with a full display of all the orisha's regalia. Each time, the shrine room is draped with rich cloths in appropriate colors. The *soperas* that contain the sacred stones are hung with sumptuous altar cloths, and the floor is arrayed with the orisha's favorite flowers, fruits, and cakes. In a prosperous pile, this regalia can be fine indeed and the sight breathtaking.[5]

I can attest to this ardently. The first *bembé* (a feast and celebration for an orisha) I attended was, in fact, for Shango's birthday at a Cuban madrina's house in The Bronx. The ceilings were very high and paneled with rich wooden carvings, elaborate cherubs and angels, but what was stunning was a mass of red, red, red glistening apples (which Shango favors) that in a pyramid seemed to reach through to the heavens. Cigars, rum, the preeminent accoutrements, his ax: the eccentricities of his paramours, Oya and Oshun, everywhere visible, fans and honey. The drums that so vexed slave owners filling the space with the power of Nommo: Being. The fullness and unknowableness of Oludamare, or as Robert Ferris Thompson says, "a flash of the spirit." Dancing, prayers, reunions spiritual and corporeal, lasting into the dawn. Till one's breath gives way with thanks.

Thank goodness that shrines for our ancestors or families aren't so overwhelming. In Skobi Matunde's *Seed of African-American People,* he brings us more down to earth, to ourselves.

Setting up a household shrine varies depending on the purpose of the shrine. They are usually for shrines remembering a particular ancestor or family member. After cleaning the area for the shrine, it is advised to be smudged with smoke from cedar sage, or aromatic smoke. Pray over the leaves and over the smudging area, asking to clean all negative vibrations and emotions. Circle the room while you offer your prayers. Then take a bowl of water and place a small amount of cologne, Florida or rose water, and add a little saliva as personal fluids. Breathe a prayer into the bowl, then sprinkle the altar area with the water. Asking your

ancestors . . . to respect and honor the libation. After this is done
place a white cloth with a candle and a glass of water and concen-
trated purpose of the shrine in prayer and meditation. The shrine
should always be placed in an area where you can pray and medi-
tate without being disturbed too much.[6]

There's in us, whether we get the Holy Ghost or not, an infinite
capacity to render the separation of soul and flesh impotent: to
claim the wholeness of our being in the same way we go about
cookin' up a storm, preparing something divine.

And then, there are God's Chosen people, Jews, who also are
present among the African-American community through con-
version or direct descent from the Falashas, who come from the
area north of what was formerly Lake Rudolph, but now and
originally Lake Turkhana in Alkebu-Lan (Ethiopia). While
slavery was a distinctive interruption in continuous practice of
Jewish laws and rituals, the people survived. According to Dr.
Ben, Yosef A. A. ben-Jachannan, black Jews rely on the same religious texts as European Jews with distinct differences in read-
ings and meanings of these texts. Falasha belief departs from European Judaic thought in this way:

> Just As The Table (Passover Seder) Is Spread With The Ritual
> Foods Of Horseradish, Wine, Matzos (unleavened bread), The
> Mixture Of Liver And Wine, The Hard Boiled Eggs, Scal-
> lions, Water Heavy With Salt, And The Good Lamb, We Are
> Reminded That The Passover (Pesach) Was Of Death And
> That The Dead Was Allowed To Remain With The Dead And
> That The Living Had To Carry On With The Living.[7]

I recall with some humility a spring in Curaçao, the Netherlands
Antilles, when Good Friday, the first day of Passover, and the
Islamic feast day of *'Iyd el Fitr* were being observed simulta-
neously. On that day this dust, cacti, and azure-tinged apricot

skies was quiet with prayers of the faithful, while I stood outside the oldest synagogue in the New World. The weight of Jews escaping the Inquisition, the mingling of all our religions and cultures, came over me like a soul being bathed in the gaze of all our lords.

The Islamic world in our hemisphere is vast and diverse, but the heart remains for all followers in the Holy Koran. What we must know, to not be philistines, is that Ramadan, which lasts from thirty to fifty days, is marked by fasting, broken traditionally after sundown with a glass of water and a date. However, at the end of Ramadan, a great feast (now this from the mouth of a young friend, Taalib' Music' Hassar) of lamb, chicken, macaroni and cheese, candy from piñatas, staged performances, stick dances, singing, dancing, a gathering for Muslims from all over come to New York. These are Black Muslims from America, vernacularly known as Yorkites, though actually from the Ansaaru Allah Community or Helpers of Allah, hosting a New World Mecca of a kind.

Couscous
Royale
3 carrots
3 zucchini
12 oz pumpkin or squash
5 cups Fresh Vegetable Stock (recipe follows)
2 cinnamon sticks, broken in half
2 tsp ground cumin
1 tsp ground coriander
Pinch saffron strands
2 tbs olive oil
Pared rind and juice of lemon

2 TBS clear honey
2 ⅔ CUPS precooked couscous
½ CUP butter or margarine, softened
I CUP large seedless raisins
Salt and pepper to taste
Fresh cilantro to garnish

Cut the carrots and zucchini into 3-inch pieces and cut in half lengthwise. Trim the pumpkin or squash and discard the seeds. Peel and cut into pieces the same size as the carrots and zucchini. Put the stock, spices, saffron, and carrots in a large saucepan. Bring to a boil, skim off any scum and add the olive oil. Simmer for 15 minutes. Add the lemon rind and juice to the pan with honey, zucchini, and pumpkin or squash. Season well. Bring to a boil and simmer 10 minutes longer. Meanwhile, soak the couscous according to packet instructions. Transfer to a steamer or large strainer lined with cheesecloth and place over the vegetable pan. Cover and steam as directed. Stir in the butter or margarine. Pile the couscous into a warm serving plate. Drain the vegetables, reserving the stock, lemon rind, and cinnamon. Arrange the vegetables on top of the couscous. Put the raisins on top and spoon over 6–8 tablespoons of reserved stock. Keep warm. Return the remaining stock to the heat and boil for 5 minutes to reduce slightly. Discard the lemon rind and cinnamon. Garnish with the cilantro and serve with the sauce separately.

This can be kept chilled for up to 3 days or frozen for up to 3 months. Do not add salt while the stock is cooking. It is better to season the stock to complement the dish in which it is to be used. Makes 6 ¼ cups.

Fresh
Vegetable
Stock

8 oz shallots
1 large carrot, diced
1 STALK celery, chopped
½ BULB fennel
1 CLOVE garlic
1 bay leaf
A few fresh parsley and tarragon/sprigs
8 ¾ CUPS water
Pepper

*Put all the ingredients in a large saucepan and bring to a boil.
Skim off the surface scum with a flat spoon, then reduce to a
gentle simmer. Cover partially and cook for 45 minutes. Leave
to cool. Line strainer with clean cheesecloth and put over a large
pitcher or bowl. Cover and store in small quantities in refrigerator or freezer.*

W. E. B. Du Bois may very well have been correct in defining
the dominant issue of the twentieth century as a matter of race,
but the idea that we, African-Americans, wrestle with a dual
identity, black and American, is now a blending or continuous
adjustment of our many identities. One thing for sure, I know
and believe in my heart, the souls of black folks are truly in many
good hands.

Epilogue

Sweets for my sweet
sugar for my honey
I'll never, ever let you go.

THE DRIFTERS,
"Sugar Pie, Honey Bunch"

In 1719 Governor Hamilton (from the Leeward Islands)
complained that slave imports had lately declined and
that slave prices had been rising, both trends proving to be
a great Hindrance to the Sugar Plantations ... Of the 41
vessels entering Antigua with slaves in 1721–27, 38 ar-
rived from the African coast and 3 from Nevis, Boston,
and Barbados.

DAVID BARRY GASPAR,
"Slave Importation, Runaways, and
Compensation in Antigua, 1720–1729,"
The Atlantic Slave Trade

WHEN I DANCED my way through my teenage
years, I always stopped to do my very fancy footwork
to The Drifters' "Sugar Pie, Honey Bunch / You
know that I love you / Can't help myself / I want you and nobody else." Of course, as a fifteen-year-old I wasn't thinking

that the consumption of sugar, itself, is a kind of addiction, nor did I consider the vicious irony that sugar-cane production fell in proportion to the development of beet sugar, which didn't require great numbers of African slave laborers at a great expense, as noted above. One of the keen marketing tools of the sugar beet farmers was to remind their dessert-craving consumers that their sugar had never been touched by black hands, which maybe made it taste better or whiter, I don't know. What I do know is that, regardless of our initial encounters with cane, we are still singing songs like *Como La India*, "*Mi querida tan dulce, tan rica*" (My beloved, so sweet, so sensuous), and asking our toddlers for some sugar, meaning "kisses."

We remain a complex people with a sweet tooth. I'd just as soon slice a mango and dice some strawberries, add a bit of grated coconut, and call it a day. I mean dessert, but I know there are some of us who must show off after the main course. I've found these receipts from the Yucatán.

Mixed Fruit in Syrup   *Set a pot to boil a little more than a cup of dark brown sugar, a quart of water, and 2 cinnamon sticks for about 20 minutes, when it begins to thicken. Add 1 whole cantaloupe, cubed and seeded, three oranges peeled and sliced horizontally, 4–5 pieces of sugar cane peeled and in thin strips, a half dozen guavas, halved and seeded. Cook on medium heat until fruits are tender, about 10–15 minutes. Take off stove. Let this cool significantly before serving.*

The Dominican Republic has a bloody as well as rich history of struggle for democracy and resolution of centuries-old conflicts with black Haitian neighbors, inescapable when we hear tales of the River of Blood, when Haitians crossing the border were butchered in a scene that's now been repeated in Rwanda and Burundi. We could even revisit the dictatorship of Trujillo and the thousands tortured and silenced, as remarkably recounted in Julia Alvarez's "Tres Mariposas," or simply push our memories to Argentina in the 1970s or the soccer stadium in Santiago with Victor Jara's voice lingering somewhere among the clouds, veering off toward horizons where our dreams still prod us through one more day.

We want to offer our children, our guests, something to relish, something that makes them smile. We could always go to the magnificent Merengue Festival in Santo Domingo and end the day gleaming with sweat and Olga Tanon's voice still electrifying our hips or Johnny Ventura seducing complete strangers to unimaginable romantic flourishes, or we could just cook something up.

Let your raisins, half a cup or so, soak in about 3 tablespoons of dark rum. Put that somewhere the children can't reach it. Then let half a loaf of hardened day-old bread soak in about 3 cups of milk (mixture of buttermilk or sweetened condensed milk will do just as well, it's your choice). After a half hour or so, add 1½ cups of sugar (white or light brown), 4 tablespoons of butter, 5 eggs slightly beaten, 1 teaspoon of vanilla extract, and a pinch of salt. Throw in your rum and raisins (you can substitute straw-

Dominican Bread Pudding

berries or peaches or just put the rum in, but if you use these reduce the amount of milk slightly) and mix thoroughly. Grease
your baking pan with butter and sprinkle some brown sugar
about it evenly, on the bottom and the sides. Place this pan in another pan of hot water to make sure nothing burns or gets uneven
while baking. Bake at 350 degrees for nearly an hour until a
straw from the broom comes out cleanly. This can be served
warm or chilled once turned over a serving dish.

Baked Papaya For those of us with more simple tastes, this dish is perfecto.
Mash the pulp of 4 ripe papayas, set this in a baking dish, and
cover with 2 cups of grated coconut. Leave that alone. Take 4
cups of milk, 1 cup of sugar, and the grated rind and juice of an
orange and boil, making a custard that we pour over the papaya
and coconut; bake at 350–375 degrees. Then, when the custard
is firm, we take it out the oven, chill, and serve.

And there's always corn bread in warm syrup or molasses. Marc
Latamie, conceptual artist and photographer from Martinique,
posed an ontologically challenging question at a conference
called The Fact of Blackness at London's Institute of Contemporary Art. While he was examining the remains of abandoned
sugar refineries and chatting with workers at the lone functioning
refinery in Martinique, he was exploring our relationship to
sugar, our purpose for being, our continued presence in this
hemisphere.

Of course. The Plantation is the reason we are in Martinique even though today nobody understands why we are there because the question is not a natural question. For the piece I made for Mirage [the exhibition at the conference], I worked with images of the last sugar factory in Martinique. I found it very interesting to see how this factory—which is still working perfectly—is trying to survive pressure from around the world regarding its product . . . I didn't want to raise the question of why sugar is no longer one of the main products in Martinique or elsewhere in the Caribbean . . . I cannot make a factory. I have no reason to make one. I try to force myself into the position of the traders. I ask them, "Why are you doing this? Why are you doing that? Why are you moving tons of sugar everyday?"[1]

Well, Latamie discovered that two of Frantz Fanon's nephews worked at the refinery, so they know why they are here in this, the New World. Yet, what about the rest of us? If we were here to produce cotton, sugar, indigo, rice, tobacco, coffee, gold, et alia, and most of us aren't doing that anymore, what are we doing here? I know the history of the world would be a contorted mess without the disciplined and rapacious drive of the slave trade. I know untold and largely unrecognized humanity were brought to realms where they were a step beyond human debris. But I also know we've done more than survive. We've found bounty in the foods the gods set before us, strength in the souls of black folks, delight in the *guele* (smell) of our sweating bodies, and beauty in Jean Toomer's image of a November cotton flower.

What and how we cook is the ultimate implication of who we are. That's why I know my God can cook—I'm not foolish enough to say I could do something the gods can't do. So if I can cook, you know God can.

Notes

INTRODUCTION
Learning to Be Hungry/ Holdin' On Together

1. Keith Antar Mason, "Mississippi Gulag," (Los Angeles, 1995, manuscript), 10.

CHAPTER 1
What'd You People Call That?

1. Gary B. Nash, *Forging Freedom, The Formation of Philadelphia's Black Community: 1720–1840* (Cambridge: Harvard University Press, 1988), 188–189.

CHAPTER 3
All It Took Was a Road/ Surprises of Urban Renewal

1. Ntozake Shange, "My Song for Hector Lavoe," *Aloud!: Voices* (New York: Henry Holt & Co., 1994), 366.

CHAPTER 4
Birthday in Brixton

1. C. L. R. James, "Orleans," from *The Black Jacobins: Toussaint L'Ouverture and the Santo Domingo Revolution,* in *The C. L. R. James Reader* (Oxford: Blackwell Press, 1993), 108.

CHAPTER 6
Brazil: More African Than Africans

1. Lygia Fagundes Telles, *The Girl in the Photograph,* translated from

the Portuguese by Margaret A. Neves (New York: Avon Books, a Bard Book, 1982), 123.

2. Ibid., 118.

CHAPTER 7
What Is It We Really Harvestin' Here?

1. Lynne Fauley Emery, *Black Dance: 1619 to Today* (Pennington, N.J.: Princeton Books, a Dance Horizon book, 1988), 27.

2. Sterling Stuckey, *Slave Culture* (New York: Oxford University Press, 1987), 65.

3. Henry Hobhouse, *Seeds of Change: Five Plants that Transformed Mankind* (New York: Harper & Row, Perennial Library, 1987), 74.

4. Ibid.

5. Karen Hess, *The Carolina Rice Kitchen: The African Connection* (Columbia: University of South Carolina Press, 1992), 13.

6. Ibid., 17.

CHAPTER 8
Westward Ho! Anywhere Must Be Better'n Here!

1. William Loren Katz, *The Early Settlers* (New York: Simon and Schuster, Touchstone Books, 1996), 176.

2. Ibid., 250.

3. Joseph M. Murphy, *Santería: African Spirits in America* (Boston: Beacon Press, 1993), 31.

4. Ibid., 19.

CHAPTER 9
Better Late Than Never

1. Charles A. Taylor, with illustrations by Charles A. Taylor II, *Juneteenth: A Celebration of Freedom* (Madison, Wisc.: Praxis Publications, African-American Celebration Series, 1995), 12.

2. *World Music: The Rough Guide*, ed. Simon Broughton et al. (London: Rough Guides, 1995), 509.

CHAPTER 10
Is That Why the Duke Had a Train of His Own?

1. Kenneth F. Kiple and Brian T. Higgins, "Mortality Caused by Dehydration during the Middle Passage," in *The Atlantic Slave Trade: Effects on Economies, Societies, and Peoples in Africa, the Americas, and Europe,* ed. Joseph E. Inkori and Stanley L. Engerman (Durham: Duke University Press, 1994), 327–328.

2. Phillipe Oszuscik, "French Creoles on the Gulf Coast," in *To Build a New Land: Ethnic Landscapes in North America,* ed. Allen G. Noble (Baltimore: Johns Hopkins University Press, 1992), 142–144.

CHAPTER 11
What Did You Serve? Oh, No, You Did Not!

1. "Calling the Ancestral Roll," in *Leaf and Bone: African-Praise Poems,* ed. Judith Gleason (New York: Penguin Books, 1994), 45.

CHAPTER 12
Virtual Realities, Real People, Real Foods

1. Wole Soyinka, "Beyond the Berlin Wall," *Transitions* 51 (1991): 21.

2. Dale T. Garden, "This City Has Too Many Slaves Joined Together: The Abolitionist Crisis in Salvador, Bahia, Brazil, 1848–1856," in *The African Diaspora,* ed. Aluisine Jalloh and Stephen E. Maizlish (College Station: Texas A & M University Press, 1996), 96.

3. Molefi Kete Asante, "The Essential Grounds," in *Afrocentricity* (Trenton, N.J.: Africa World Press, 1996), 22–23.

4. Lynne Fauley Emery, *Black Dance: 1619 to Today* (Pennington, N.J.: Princeton Books, a Dance Horizon book, 1988), 30.

5. Joseph M. Murphy, *Santería: African Spirits in America* (Boston: Beacon Press, 1993), 56.

6. Skobi Matunde, *Seed of African-American People,* 202–203.

7. Yosef A. A. ben-Jachannan, *We, the Black Jews,* vol. 1 and vol. 2 (Baltimore: Black Classic Press, 1993), 156.

EPILOGUE

1. Marc Latamie, "Artists' Dialogue," in *The Fact of Blackness: Frantz Fanon and Visual Representation*, ed. Alan Read (London: Institute of Contemporary Arts, Institute of International Visual Arts; Seattle: Bay Press, 1996), 152–153.

Credits

Acknowledgments

Although this book has been a challenge and a pleasure to write, I've not done it alone. I must thank my editor, Tisha Hooks, for her patience, humor, and acute sense of continuity as well as my agents, Joe Regal and Timothy Seldes, of Russell and Volkening, Inc., for dealing with my fits of revelations about food, family, and self.

Certainly, I have to add the inspiration and quiet of the Atlantic Center for the Arts, Philadelphia's Freedom Theatre Writer-in-Residence Program, the Ensemble Theatre of Houston, and Crossroads Theatre of New Brunswick, where, as an associate artist, I am afforded technical and intellectual support whether my project is to hit the boards or the kitchen.

To my mother, Eloise Owens Williams, without whom I'd have no idea how to get around a kitchen, I give ten thousand hugs, kisses, and a Carolinian slap on the back. To my grandmothers, Viola and Ida, all my aunts, Margaret, Emma, Thelma, Vera, and Billye, I owe a wealth of memories that created my love of our cooking and the love that passes our ways of caring about one another along from one generation to the next. I am indebted to my sisters, Ifa Bayeza, Bisa Williams-Manigualt, and Amiée Felder-Williams, to my cookin' crazy brother, Paul T. Williams, Esq., and I hope I'm doing the same for my wondrous daughter, Savannah, who tasted, tested, researched, and ate leftovers from Texas to Chicago while I finished "our" project.

Many, many friends assisted and lent shoulders to lean on or cans of Easy-Off along with family secrets and common sense. I'm thinking of Miguel and Irma Algarin, Hailma Taha, Marie Grant, the Calloways, Melvin Glover, Dena Swayze, Molly Stevenson of the American Cowboy Museum in Houston, Anna Maria Turner, Gary Cruz, "Music," Nisa Ra of the Bird of Paradise, and Yvette Smalls, Renée Thompson, Merilene Williams, and Eddie Rouse, Mickey Davidson and the PrescottRichardson family of Carolina, Puerto Rico, and The Bronx, poets and actors who kept me company in the kitchen or at the computer station as I metaphorically gorged my palate and imagination, and helped me remember how to hold normal conversations.

My research assistants, Anjela Byer and Denise Baron, were integral to the development of this book, as was my literary dramaturge Enomoyi Ama of the University of Texas, whose sense of my visions and meticulous mind-set helped me maintain focus. I must also thank the staff of the Philadelphia Free Library for making available obscure and peculiar texts I'd sometimes request.

I want, especially, to thank Juan Daniel Rosado y Clark for those predawn wake-up calls and late-night assurances that I wasn't losing my mind, but the oven should really be preheated before I took time to be nostalgic about Blanchisseuse, Trinidad. I wish I could thank my father, Paul Towbin Williams, M.D., in person for trying everything I ever cooked, even though he believed I spiced things up too much and didn't cook vegetables long enough.

To my doctor, John Wootten, my analyst, Anthony Molino,

and my friend Dr. Robert Bacon, I can finally offer platters of delicacies that are not as ephemeral as dreams.

I thank the spirits that guide and protect me for sustaining and feeding me.